LISA SUZANNE

CLEAN BREAK
A Little Like Destiny Book THREE

Published in the United States of America by Books by LS, LLC.

ISBN-13: 978-1979020343
ISBN-10: 1979020345

Content Editing: It's Your Story Content Editing
Proofreading: Proofreading by Katie
Cover Design: Najla Qamber Designs
Cover Photograph: Eric Battershell
Cover Model: Mike Chabot

CLEAN
Break

books by Lisa Suzanne

A Little Like Destiny: The Complete Series

A Little Like Destiny

Only Ever You

Clean Break

The Invisible Thread Duet

The Power to Break

The Invisible Thread

The Truth and Lies Duet

It Started with a Lie

It Ended with the Truth

Visit Lisa on Amazon for more titles

dedication

To the two boys who have given me my happily ever after.

one

"What are you doing here?" Mark asks. I almost stand up to see who's there, but I realize the couch is hiding me. If it's Brian, I don't want him to know I've been up here with his brother.

"Looking for you." Brian's voice cuts through the night, and my heart races.

"Why?"

I hear a laugh, and I can picture Brian's cocky smile. "I think it's time we had a talk."

Mark steps around the couch without looking down at me, without drawing attention to the fact that I'm here.

"About what?" Mark asks.

"You know what," Brian mutters.

I freeze on the couch as I strain to hear what they're saying without making a sound. I'm terrified Brian's going to step around the couch and find me here. He can't find out about Mark and me, not this way—especially not if I want to try to fix things between us.

"Are you drunk?" Mark asks.

There's a beat of silence and I remember Mark telling me that Brian tends to make bad decisions when he drinks.

"Yeah. So?" There's a short pause and some rustling, then Brian says, "Did you think I wouldn't find out?"

"Find out what?" Mark asks.

"About the two of you fucking each other behind my back."

My heart stops as an icy fear filters through my veins.

He knows.

I consider getting up from the spot where I sit on the couch. Brian already knows about Mark and me. I might as well stop hiding now, both literally and figuratively. It's over with Mark, anyway.

Mark doesn't deny anything, though he doesn't admit to it, either. Instead, he takes a chance by tossing out an accusation. "You don't want to marry Reese."

"No, I don't." Brian laughs, and it's a snide, vicious sound I've never heard from him before. "But it's worth it to see you suffer. You should've seen your dumb ass in the backseat of the car when I brought it up."

No, I don't. His words grate on my mind and reverberate through my entire being. I start to vibrate with confusion as it seeps into my pores.

"You know what's the best part of all this?" Brian asks, slurring on the *s* sounds in his words.

"What's that?"

"Your voice on replay from that night in my head. *This girl's different.*" His voice goes up a few octaves and drips with sarcasm. "*Tonight meant something to me.* Blah-de-fucking-blah." Brian laughs, and the sound is harsh and grating. Mean.

"Is that supposed to be me?" Mark asks.

"It's you acting like a pussy the night you met her."

My heart races. Mark told Brian about me?

"You remembered her?" Mark asks.

"Of course I did. You think I'm gonna forget about the girl my brother said has the potential to change the course of his life? I ran into her the next morning when she was getting off the elevator."

"And that was it?"

"Well, no. I had to do some handiwork with the principal of her school to make sure Reese would be the one who came begging for a donation. A little research goes a long way, though, and I snagged her pretty easily after that. Throw a little cash around, and they drop right to their knees, eh?" He pauses, and his voice is nasty when he speaks again. "I learned that from my big brother."

A wave of nausea washes over me. I feel like I might be sick right here on the couch as I listen to this garbage, as my heart fills with hatred for the man who was just talking to me about marriage a few hours ago.

"Destiny dropped her right into my lap," Brian says, using the code word Mark and I share, "and I'm not talking about the same Destiny whose G-string I was sticking dollar bills into last weekend."

"You went to a strip club last weekend?"

Brian grates out another harsh laugh. "Every weekend I'm out of town. It's a business expense."

My chest tightens and my breathing labors as tears prick behind my eyes. I shouldn't feel spurned after cheating on him with Mark, but his words cut into my ribs with a sharpness that nauseates me.

"What the hell is wrong with you?" Mark asks.

"It's sweet. Revenge, I mean. It tastes good. Almost as good as Reese's cunt."

"Why'd you go after her if you knew I wanted more than one night?" Mark's voice is broken.

"Let's use our fucking heads here, big brother."

It's quiet for a beat. "Kendra," Mark murmurs.

"Bingo."

I hear someone blow out a breath.

"You're fucking sick," Mark says.

I can picture Brian's cocky smirk, but neither of them speaks for a minute.

"Why are you telling me this now?" Mark asks.

"It's time to end the charade. With what happened to Pops, I realized life is short. I don't want to waste time anymore, though she is a sweet fuck. I did what I needed to. I got my revenge. It's time to move on. You can have her if you still want her." It's quiet for a beat, then Brian asks, "You tapped that bareback yet?"

"Fuck you," Mark spits out.

"She rode me bare and she felt like a fucking velvet piece of heaven. You should try it sometime."

The sound of a sack of potatoes falling to the ground greets my ears, and I can't take it anymore. I stand up and turn around to see what's going on.

Brian is on the ground, completely defenseless and obviously drunk as Mark straddles his waist and pummels him, punching his jaw with one fist and his nose with the other. Brian's reflexes are slowed from the alcohol.

I've never seen an actual fight in person—even fights on television give me anxiety—but this isn't much of a fight. It's a defenseless man who's had far too much to drink getting bashed by a man who bears a grudge.

Fresh blood glints in the moonlight on Brian's face, and a new wave of nausea passes over me.

Mark sees me frozen in place on the other side of the couch. I should run over there, grab his arms, stop him from hurting his brother further. There will be ramifications to this—of that I'm sure. But I don't know how to stop him, and I don't know if I want to. From my perspective, Brian deserves worse than a few hits to the face.

Mark's eyes are full of raw anger, but when they meet mine, they refocus and soften. He pauses in his pursuit of beating the shit out of his brother.

"This one's for you," Mark whispers, then he backhands his brother across the face, leading with his knuckles. Brian spits out a mouthful of blood as Mark stands, opens the door, and walks down the stairs leading back to his penthouse.

two

Soft moaning greets my ears, and I stand stock still as I stare at the door Mark just disappeared through. Brian groans softly, and I'm faced with a decision—another in a long string of them. Each one I've made lately seems to be the wrong one, and I'm certain whatever I do this time won't yield a different result.

Do I help the man bleeding from the face all over the rooftop?

Or do I go back down to the man who just beat the shit out of his brother in some convoluted attempt to defend my honor?

My heart longs for Mark, needs to talk to him about everything that just happened, wants to make sure he's okay after losing his grandfather, his brother, and me—all in very different ways and all in the span of a few hours.

I'm so fraught with confusion that the thought enters my mind that maybe he didn't lose *me* in that equation.

But the girl from Sevens...the pictures he admitted were real. The words he said about how I'm better off without him.

Those take up the forefront of my mind. And then my brain registers that the man on the ground moaning in drunken pain probably requires medical attention.

Despite the confession Brian just made to his brother that he never loved me, that he only pursued a relationship with me because he wanted revenge on his brother, I can't just leave a man bleeding all over the ground. My conscience won't allow it even if I believe he got what he deserved.

Deep down, though, I can't truly believe what he said to his brother was true. I refuse to believe he's so bent on revenge that he'd use me in such an evil way for such a long time. He's related to Mark and Lizzie, and they're good people—there must be some good somewhere inside him.

He's drunk. He's hurting—his grandfather died and his girlfriend cheated on him with his brother. He said things he'll regret in the morning—we all might've.

I take my time dialing my phone for emergency services. It's hard to feel bad for Brian when I'm battling my own internal rage over his words.

"Nine-one-one, what's your emergency?"

My immediate instinct is to protect Mark. "I found a man badly beaten. He needs medical help."

"Is he breathing?"

"Yes."

"Is he conscious?"

I glance down at the drunk man moaning on the ground. "Yes."

"Can you give me an address and a callback number?"

I give the dispatcher the information, and then she asks the one question I'm not real sure how to answer.

"What suite number?"

I can't say we're on the roof. Despite the confusion clouding my head, one thing is clear. Mark is the only tenant with access, and he'll immediately be brought in for questioning. That'll be all over the news in seconds.

"He's, um...down near the front entrance." I'll figure out a way to get him there before they arrive.

"What happened?"

"Uh," I say, stalling as I form a lie. "I don't know."

"An ambulance is on its way." She asks more questions, but I'm trying to figure out how the hell to get him off this roof. He's still conscious, but he's definitely drunk and there's blood everywhere as it pours out of his nose and from his lip. I get off the phone and glance around.

Part of me wants to go get Mark and tell him to clean up his own damn mess, but he shouldn't. He's got too much to lose and there's too much at stake for him to get involved, especially now that I've called the paramedics.

"Brian," I say. He groans. I step over toward him. "Brian?" I repeat. I nudge him a little with my foot, leery to get too close to the blood pooling around him.

I hate seeing him like this. This is the man I thought I was in love with, the man I thought owned my heart, the one I started picturing a future with. This is the man I thought was the secure, safe, logical choice. Yet here he lies on the ground, suddenly not at all the man I thought he was, and despite everything that's happened, my heart breaks a little more.

I kneel beside him. He looks worse up close than he did from a few feet away, and I fight the nausea I feel at the sight of all this blood glistening in the moonlight way too close to me.

"Can you stand up?" I ask, keeping my voice soft. "I'm gonna get you some help, but I need you to stand up. I need you to help me."

He grunts out some unintelligible sound. I pull on his arm, but I think he might've passed out. I'm not sure if it's from the alcohol or from the beating he just got. I look around desperately, hopeful there might be something up here that can help me but sure there isn't as my heart races.

I yank on his arm some more. If I can drag him over to the elevator, I can get him downstairs and off this godforsaken rooftop.

I pull on his arm as hard as I can, but he barely budges. He's deadweight and I don't have the strength to move him.

I text Mark because I don't know what else to do, who else to contact, where else to turn.

Me: *I need to get him off the roof. I need your help.*

I wait all of three seconds before I realize he's not going to respond. Of course he won't. He's not just pissed at his brother for what he did—he's hurting because of everything that went down today, and the way he sees it, Brian got exactly what he deserved.

Protecting Mark right now is the least I can do.

Lizzie.

Her name pops into my head as the answer. She's the only person I can think to call.

"Reese?" she answers.

"Lizzie, I need your help."

"What's wrong?"

"Mark beat the shit out of Brian and we're on Mark's roof. Brian's drunk and passed out and I called an ambulance and I don't know how to get him off the roof."

"Jesus Christ," she mutters. "When did you call the ambulance?"

"Just now."

"Okay, listen carefully. I'll call Vinny. Stay out of it. Go down to Mark's condo right now. You shouldn't be there when the ambulance shows."

"Why not?"

"We're wasting time. I need to call Vinny."

She cuts the call and I stand there wondering what the hell just happened. I can't just leave him here all alone. Who knows how much he had to drink? Who knows the extent of his injuries? He needs someone with him. As much as I hate him for using me—and keeping Mark and me apart—he's still a human being, and my sympathy wins.

I stay with him until my phone rings.

I glance at the screen before I answer. "Lizzie, what's going on?"

"Vinny was down in Mark's lobby. He's on his way up."

"Thank you."

"I'm serious, Reese. Don't go to the hospital. Get out of there. Let Vinny handle it."

Why? I want to scream the single word, but I'm desperate for a solution to this huge problem. "As soon as he gets up here, I'll go back to Mark's place."

"Is he okay?"

"Brian? I think so. He's bleeding a lot and smells like a bar, but I think he'll be okay."

"Physical wounds will heal. I was talking about Mark."

"Oh." My heart bleeds for Mark. "I don't know. He took off."

"What happened?"

"Brian stumbled up here and spouted a bunch of shit to Mark about how he's been using me because he knew Mark had feelings for me after our one night together."

"Are you serious?"

I don't respond—I can't, because the elevator doors open and Vinny comes barreling out of it. "I'll call you back," I say in to the phone.

I end the call. "Over here," I yell, and Vinny runs across the rooftop toward us.

"This was Mark's doing?" he asks.

"Yes."

"Good work," he says as he looks down at Brian for a minute and admires Mark's handiwork. He raises both brows like he's impressed. "He'll be fine. I'll take it from here."

"Thank you, Vinny." I have the urge to rush into his arms and hug him.

He doesn't respond as he gets down and heaves Brian up over his shoulder. Blood splatters drip from his face as Vinny carries him over toward the elevator like he weighs nothing when I couldn't even nudge his body to get him up.

Thank God for Vinny.

three

When I open the door leading from the stairwell back into Mark's condo, I don't know what to expect. We already declared we were over, but that was before Brian's big confession. Now that we know Brian was purposely keeping the two of us apart, we're free to be together.

If only it was that simple.

Mark was the one who pushed me away. He pushed me back into Brian's arms.

I wander toward the bedroom I share with Brian and start packing my bag without even thinking. I'm numb as I go through the motions. I half expect to turn around and find Mark standing in the doorway silently watching me, but when I turn around, no one's there.

You don't want to be with someone like me, and I don't deserve to be with someone like you.

I still don't know what he meant when he told me I don't want to be with someone like him. Why wouldn't I want to be with someone like him? He may be flawed, but I love him—flaws and all. I love the past that has shaped him. I love the fact that he puts everyone else first. Even when he beat the shit out of his brother, he still put me first when he delivered that final blow. *This one's for you.*

I'd give up everything to make it work with him. I'd quit my job and give up the house I share with Jill and take up a nomadic lifestyle to travel the road with Vail.

I'm just not convinced love is enough.

It's not just Mark and me anymore, anyway. It's his whole family. Whether or not they accept me or like me, they've grown to know me as Brian's girlfriend. Their mother comes to mind first. I can't imagine the sort of hatred Diane will spew at me when she finds out one of her boys knocked the other one's teeth in because of *me*.

Maybe she never has to know, and maybe it doesn't matter anyway.

I glance around the bedroom. Brian's bag is tucked neatly in the corner, a stark reminder of everything that has changed in the last hour. I can't stay here, certainly not in this particular bedroom.

I dial Lizzie's number again.

"I know we don't know each other that well, but I don't know what else to do. Can I come stay with you?" I ask the question after she barely greets me.

"Of course you can," she says, her voice gentle. "Get your stuff and meet me downstairs. I'll be there in ten minutes."

"Thank you," I whisper. I can't say it out loud because of the tears that have already started burning their way down my cheeks.

I toss the remainder of my belongings in my duffel bag, and even as I do it, I can't help but think how none of this is actually mine. Mark had someone purchase everything for me when we dropped what we were doing in the back of a Yukon in Los Angeles to trek to Chicago. It seems like another lifetime when that happened, not just a few days.

Even though what we were doing was wrong back then, it was so much simpler. I was going to end things with Brian as soon as I saw him so Mark and I could be together, and now I'm not with either of them. Confusion lies at the heart of every move I make, and I think some distance from this place will do me good.

Too bad I picked their sister's place as my sanctuary.

Lizzie's in pajama pants and a tank top when her car pulls up in front of Mark's place. I get into the car and set the duffel on my lap. I didn't see Mark before I walked out. I don't know if he's somewhere in his condo or if his hands are busted up from kicking his brother's ass or if he's off kissing some random girl in a back alley behind a bar.

His hands.

I hope he didn't hurt them when he was smashing his brother's face. I wonder when his next show is, whether his hands will be strong enough to play guitar or if they'll need time to heal.

"Thanks for picking me up," I say softly.

She doesn't respond, but she does set her hand on my arm. It's a friendly gesture, and it makes me feel like everything's going to be okay.

We pull up in front of another skyscraper after a few minutes, and she leaves her car in the valet lane before we walk together into the building. We head up in the elevator, and when she opens the front door to her place, I immediately see how different her place is from her brother's.

Family photos are all over the place. Everywhere I look, I see an eight-by-ten smile of Mark's or a five-by-seven cocky grin of Brian's. Family vacations, family dinners, family pictures in front of a fireplace at casa de Fox on Christmas morning. There are other pictures, too—pictures of Dave's family, I assume. Lizzie's in some of them and not in others.

It's overwhelming, but it shows me how much she loves her stupid brothers.

I chuckle at one photo of a younger Mark and Brian standing next to huge costumed characters of Beavis and Butt-head. Lizzie stands in the middle with a wide grin.

Dave is sitting in a recliner in the family room with ESPN blaring in front of him. He turns off the television when we walk in.

"Is everything okay?" he asks.

Lizzie looks at me, and I lift a shoulder. "I don't know."

"You want to talk about what happened?" she asks. She sits on the couch and gestures for me to sit beside her. I set my bag on the floor and take a seat on the couch.

"You have too much you're dealing with, Lizzie. You don't need me to pile on top of it."

"It's a distraction," she says sadly. "Besides, you're already here, and I need to make sure my idiot brothers are okay. Start from the beginning."

I'm not even sure what to consider *the beginning*, so I start from tonight. "I was up on Mark's roof. We talked. He kept pushing me toward Brian, so finally I told him I couldn't do this back and forth thing with him anymore. I told him what he wanted to hear—that I'd forget about him and focus on my relationship with Brian."

"Wait a second," Dave interrupts, lowering his recliner so he's sitting up. "What?"

"Oh, yeah," Lizzie says dismissively. "Mark's in love with her. Didn't I tell you that?"

His eyes widen. "Uh, no, you didn't."

"Yeah, they had this thing before she met Brian. Anyway," she looks over at me, ignoring the look of shock on her future husband's face. "Continue."

I blow out a breath. "Brian came up to the roof."

"And Mark punched him?" Dave asks.

I shake my head. "Not yet. He didn't see me. Brian said he'd been using me to get back at Mark." I look at Lizzie. "Turns out you were right."

"Kendra?" Lizzie guesses.

I nod. "Brian said some nasty things, private things. Mark must've caught him off guard, and when I turned around, Mark was beating the shit out of him."

Lizzie lets out a breath. "Not the first time that's happened."

"They do this?"

Her eyes dart over to Dave, and they both nod. "Yeah, they do this. Brian gets stupid drunk and mouths off. Mark explodes because he holds it all in for too long. Usually Brian is lucid enough to fight back."

"Not tonight," I say.

She shakes her head. "Brian doesn't deal well with emotions. He's hurting because of Pops."

"He told Mark that was why he decided to come clean. He got his revenge."

"So now what?" Lizzie asks.

"Now I go home. I need to get out of here, away from both of them."

She shakes her head. "You need to stay right here."

I raise both brows as my eyes dart to hers.

"Mark's hurting, too. He may have taken his anger out on Brian, but it doesn't change anything. It doesn't fix anything. He needs you."

"I'm just supposed to show up to the funeral and hold Mark's hand instead of Brian's?" The funeral isn't for three more days. Lizzie wants me to stay here for three more days, and all I want to do is go home right the fuck now.

She shrugs. "Something like that." We're all quiet for a beat, then she takes my hand in hers. "I need you here, too. We barely know each other, but you somehow feel like a sister to me."

My eyes lift to hers. That wasn't something I ever expected to hear. I chuckle. "God, your mom already hates me. Imagine what she'll think now."

"She doesn't hate you. She's always like that with Brian's girlfriends. No one will ever be good enough for him."

"But she's not like that with Mark's girlfriends?"

"Mark doesn't do the girlfriend thing."

"He's never had one?"

She lifts a shoulder. "Maybe he has, but not anybody he ever cared to introduce to the rest of us."

"So he's always been this way." I say it flatly even though it's a question.

Lizzie lifts a shoulder but doesn't answer. Her phone starts ringing, and she looks at the screen. "It's Vinny." She picks up the call. "Hi Vinny." She's quiet as she listens, and then she blows out a breath. "A hotel would be better." She looks over at Dave, and he nods. They have that whole silent communication thing down, and I'm over here wondering what the hell they're saying to each other. "That's fine. I'll meet you downstairs."

She hangs up and stares into space for a beat.

"Is he okay?" I finally ask.

"Yeah. They're releasing him. Vinny's dropping him here then going back to check on Mark."

"Here?" I practically screech. I just can't get away from Brian no matter how hard I try, but he belongs here more than I do. "I'll get a hotel. I shouldn't be here."

Lizzie grabs my wrists. "Don't be silly. It's going to be fine, Reese. He has a concussion and a broken nose. Someone needs to watch him overnight and it's historically been me anyway. He'll stay with Mom and Dad until the funeral. This is for just one night."

Just one night. That's all it was supposed to be with Mark and me, too, and now look where we are.

The thought of just one night with either of the Fox brothers terrifies me.

Lizzie shows me to the bedroom where I'll be staying. It's a few doors away from the bedroom where Brian will be staying. I hope and pray he'll be long gone by the time I emerge from my bedroom in the morning.

But the way I hope things will work out is rarely the way it actually goes.

four

I tiptoe to the bathroom in the morning, hoping not to wake anyone up. I couldn't sleep knowing Mark is out there somewhere hurting. Is he alone? Did he find the woman from Sevens? Did he find someone new? I heard Brian come in, heard some muttering and bumbling around. He was on the other side of the wall, sleeping just a few feet away.

Is he okay? Is he in pain? Does he remember what he said to Mark? Does he know I heard everything?

Questions plagued me throughout the night as I stared up at the ceiling in Lizzie's guest room.

I checked my phone every few minutes as I willed it to notify me of a new text from Mark that never came. Is he as shattered as I am—even more because he lost his grandfather on top of everything else?

I look at the last text I sent him. It's not even about us. It's about Brian, and the signal that sends breaks my heart.

I draft a hundred different text messages to send him, but I don't even know what to say at this point.

I want to be what he needs me to be, but I'm so terrified our ship has sailed and I completely missed the boat. I keep thinking how we got so close, so goddamn fucking close, only to blow our chance completely.

I take a shower and pull on the clothes Mark's assistant arranged to have purchased for me. I don't even have my own things here. Sure, these are mine...but they're not. They're tainted with everything that's happened, and they feel heavy as they cover my skin.

When I emerge from the bathroom, Brian is passing in front of it. A shudder of anxiety darts through my whole being.

I was hoping to avoid him—hoping he wouldn't even know I was here. I don't want to see him or face the words he spoke last night. I'm sure he still has no idea that I overheard everything he said. He was too out of it after Mark beat the shit out of him to have any concept that I was the one who helped get him off the roof and to the hospital.

He looks terrible as his eyes meet mine. I gasp as I take in the extent of his injuries. Both of his eyes are shadowed with dark, black bruises. His nose is a little crooked, and he has cuts above both eyes and on both cheeks. His bottom lip is fat as it sticks out as a pillow for his top lip to rest upon.

"Reese," he says, a hint of surprise in his tone. His eyes soften beneath the dark bruises as he reaches for me, confirmation that he's keeping up the act. He has no idea that I know, and it cracks my heart a little more.

I stiffen. "Don't." My voice comes out hard and firm, and his brows furrow.

"I feel like shit this morning. A hug from my girl will do me a world of good."

I lift a finger and point at him. "Don't you dare call me your girl."

He takes a step back. "Excuse me?"

"I know everything," I hiss. "As far as I'm concerned, you got what you deserved." I move to pass him, but he grabs me by the elbow.

"What are you talking about, sweetheart?" he asks.

I shake my head as I wrestle my arm from his grasp. "You're gonna play like you're the innocent one? Bullshit."

"What?"

"God, you don't even remember. I was there last night. I heard you tell Mark you've been using me. So if you think you can stand there and *sweetheart* your way out of this one, you're delusional."

"I'm sure I said some things I didn't mean, but I love you, Reese."

My jaw drops open. "You don't have any idea what *love* is. If you did, you'd have let Mark and me have a shot instead of stepping in and messing everything up from the start."

I walk away from him toward the bedroom Lizzie called mine. I start looking for hotels on my phone, and, thankfully, he doesn't chase after me.

Trying to book a hotel for the same day is both stupid and expensive. I can't afford a hotel in downtown Chicago, just as much as I can't afford a flight back home. I open my bank app next. My big summer paycheck has dwindled. I wish I would've taken the *pumpkins* Brian offered me after his night of gambling, the same night we shared our first kiss. Two thousand bucks would come in handy right about now, but I'd been so adamant that the money was his. Looking back, now I think it was the least he could've done considering his plan to use me in his ploy to break his brother.

I'm stuck. I don't even know how to get home. I could ask Lizzie for help, but she's the one who insisted I stay here. Besides, I've already asked enough of her. She's been so gracious considering I'm in the middle of the shit between her brothers. I don't deserve to have her treat me so well—to treat me like an actual friend.

I give up on the hotel search. Anything nearby is over three hundred dollars, and I don't know the city well enough to book one of the more affordable ones. Instead, I start typing his name into my search bar. I can't seem to help myself.

Mark Ashton.

I click *News* next.

I don't find anything from the last twenty-four hours, just the same images Jill sent me yesterday morning. Images that still break my heart. Images he acknowledged were real—and while he may have told me most of what's posted online about him isn't true, he admitted that those pictures are. How am I supposed to know the difference?

I hate the images that are burned into my brain of him kissing someone else when he promised it was only me.

I hate *him*.

But I also love him with a deep and consuming fire that burns from the inside out. My broken heart is in his hands despite everything. I need to talk to him, I just don't know how. He's as unattainable to me now as he was before I even met him.

A knock at my door sends me into a panic. What if it's Brian? I can't imagine he'd even bother knocking, to be honest.

"Come in," I say as I set my phone on the nightstand.

Lizzie pops her head in. "You sleep okay?"

"Yeah," I lie. "Great, thanks."

"You hungry? Need anything?" She steps fully into the room and shuts the door behind her. She looks tired, which makes sense since she had to get up every two hours to check on Brian.

"I ran into Brian a few minutes ago," I say softly.

She winces. "How'd it go?"

I lift a shoulder but don't respond. What's there to say?

"I'm sorry. He'll be out tonight. Next on the agenda is figuring out where the hell Mark is so the two of you can talk."

I press my lips together. "He's done with me, Liz." My words come out softly as I stare down at the comforter and fight the tears pressing hotly behind my lids.

"Stop it," she says. "You weren't there that night when he was fighting his feelings for you. I promise you, Reese. He's not done."

She's been right about everything else so far, but this one's harder to buy.

***

It's later that afternoon when a text buzzes through on my phone.

Mary: *Destiny.*

My heart races. I don't even know how to get to his place, but he sends another text before I have the chance to tell him that.

Mary: *Todd will be downstairs in five minutes to pick you up.*

I want to ask if I should bring my duffel bag, if this is going to be an overnight thing, if this is cause for celebration. I don't ask, though, and I don't bring it. I don't want to come across as presumptuous.

Me: *See you soon.*

After I send the text, I change his contact information back to *Mark* in my phone. I have nothing to hide from anybody.

A black Yukon rolls up to the curb just as I walk out the front doors of Lizzie's building. I recognize Todd as he ushers me into the backseat, and then we're on our way to Mark's.

It's only a ten-minute drive, but it's ten fretful minutes filled with anxious thoughts and nervous energy. Part of me is thrilled to see him—to hold him in my arms again, to tell him how much I love him and need him, to kiss him and be the rock he needs right now.

But the other part of me is terrified. Last night before Brian's big confession, we said things to each other that meant the end of us, and I still have the other woman in those pictures to consider.

Each second that drags me closer to his building pushes another tingle of fear through me. By the time we arrive, my entire body is a mass of anxious prickles.

The doorman greets me and I spot Vinny standing next to the elevator. I walk toward him. He nods in greeting, inserts a key into the keypad in the elevator, and leaves me to ride up alone.

I knock on Mark's door once the elevator lets me off on his floor, my heart pounding so loudly I feel it in my ears. He doesn't answer even though he's expecting me. I try the handle, and the door opens.

"Hello?" I call. I step through the door and close it behind me. I lock it for good measure, then turn to walk through the huge, quiet condo toward the door that will take me to the roof. Each step of my foot causes my heart to pound just a little harder. I'm not sure why I'm filled with sudden nerves. This is a good thing. Mark wants to see me. He reached out to me for the first time since he thought I chose Brian.

This is where we make up. I decide to push out the nerves and replace them with a solid helping of hope.

I'm met with a mixture of memories when I step out onto the roof. Some are good, like the night Mark told me about where he drew the inspiration for the Vail song "Fading Tower." Others aren't so good, like last night when Mark broke his brother's nose.

I spot him right away, and the very second I see his posture, fear races down my spine. Just the way he stands tells me this isn't the happy reunion I'd hoped for.

His hands are gripping the handrail as he looks out over the buildings that inspired the song he wrote. His right hand is bandaged with gauze around his knuckles, but his left isn't. His head is bent forward, his shoulders sloping down like he has the weight of the world on him, and he looks lost in thought.

I walk up beside him quietly and place my hands on the cool metal handrail.

"Hi," I say softly.

He draws in a deep breath. This is where I expect him to look at me, to give me some indication that we're going to be okay. He keeps his eyes forward, and the fear transforms to a shudder of dread that spreads through my chest. "Hey."

I study his profile. His green eyes that normally look at me with such warmth stare straight ahead, and they're hard and icy. He doesn't look like the man I've come to know. Something's changed, something in his expression, and I don't know what it is. He's back to being the inaccessible rock star he always was despite everything we've been through together, and I'm terrified I've lost him for good this time.

He runs a hand through his hair and down the side of his stubble. It should be my hand there, my palm against his cheek as I comfort him and hold him.

Instead, I'm gripping the handrail with white knuckles as I brace myself for the worst.

He steps away from the railing and walks over to the couch. I turn to watch him, expecting him to sit, but he doesn't. Instead, he picks up a piece of paper and hands it to me.

I glance down at it. "What's this?"

"It's a first-class ticket back to Vegas. I had Vick schedule you a flight tonight."

I stare at the paper and then look up at him, my brows furrowed in total confusion. What about the funeral? Does he have work in Vegas? Why aren't we just taking his plane back?

"Thank you," I say instead of asking those questions. "Will your plane stay here?"

His brows draw in for a beat in confusion, then understanding seems to dawn. He nods. "Yes. With me."

"You're not going back to Vegas with me?"

He shakes his head, and the fear and anxiety that planted roots in my stomach start to bloom in my blood. My heart pounds.

"Why not?"

He blows out a breath and sets his hands back on the rail as his gaze falls back to the buildings. "I want to say it's because I have work in LA after the funeral and I have to go to New York to meet with label executives in a few days."

"You *want* to say that?"

His head moves up and down. "It's all true. But there's something else."

My heart, the same one that just started mending itself back together with the hope we had a chance, gains a brand-new fissure at his statement.

"What is it?" I ask. My fingers grip the handrail so hard they start to ache.

"I love you, Reese." His voice is soft and laced with pain. He doesn't look at me, instead keeping his eyes focused on the buildings in front of him as he delivers the words that'll replay in my head for many nights to come. "But love's not enough. I feel like shit about what went down last night. I need to put my family first right now, especially with the funeral in a couple days, and I can't do that and be with you."

The heat that stings behind my eyes tips over and tears wet my cheeks as they stream down my face. My chest burns and my stomach hurts as I stare at the back of the man I love.

I don't know what to say. I don't know how to tell him this is wrong, that we belong together. How do you fight someone who wants to put his family first? Of course family comes first. I just thought I was becoming part of that family for him.

Now, though, I'm sure I'm not.

He finally faces me. He runs his thumb along my cheek, catching one of my tears, and then he pulls me against him and

I sob outright. Low wails accompany my tears as my fragile heart is fully decimated.

I came here expecting a reunion, but I'll leave with a hole in my chest and aching disappointment swimming through my blood.

I breathe him in, memorizing the sandalwood and the feel of his arms wrapped around me as he comforts me after his harsh words.

"This is the hardest thing I've ever had to do," he whispers.

I look up at him through watery eyes. "Then why are you doing it?" I ask. I want to know why our love isn't enough—why I'm not enough.

He kisses me softly, and when he breaks the kiss, he leans his forehead against mine. "Because I have to. I can't see any way to make this work."

My chest aches at his words, but I don't know what to say to convince him otherwise.

He takes my hand and we walk together toward the stairs to his condo. We both move slowly, like this isn't something either of us wants, yet we can't change it. I wish I had the magical answer, the one thing that would fix all this, but I don't.

Mark freezes just outside the hallway that leads toward his bedroom. We both glance in that direction and then I feel his eyes on me as the tears continue to race down my cheeks.

I want to go in his bedroom with him, to show him how I feel about him, to find a way to change his mind.

His breath catches in his throat as our eyes meet, and I watch as the emotions play out on his expression. This is just as hard for him as it is for me. I see the pain there, feel his heartbreak in my chest like it's my own heart, damaged beyond repair now. He clears his throat but doesn't say anything, and I know it's his way of asking me into his bedroom.

My head screams *no* as I stare down at the first-class ticket in my hand. It's wrong. It'll only fuck further with my emotions. I'm upset over the other woman, the things left unexplained, the words left unsaid. I'm devastated that he's ending what we have.

But my heart speaks louder, and my heart can't say no to him. It's just like that first night we met. I couldn't leave Mandalay Bay without my shot with him, and this is my last chance to be with him one final time. My only chance to say goodbye.

It might fuck with my emotions, but I need this. I need to feel him one last time. I need to know the connection I felt with him was real.

"Will you please come with me?" he asks softly.

I don't respond with words; instead, I merely nod.

The shades are drawn. We're just two shadows moving in darkness. We stop beside the bed, and he takes my face between his warm, talented hands, the gauze on his right hand rough against my cheek.

He cups my face and lowers his mouth to mine. He opens my mouth with his tongue, kissing me desperately as tears fall down my cheeks. I wrap my arms around his waist and feel him tremble beneath my touch.

I taste the sting of salt in our kiss as my tears mingle with his, which only makes me hurt more for what we're giving up.

We slowly undress each other through quiet moans of pleasure and soft lamentations of loss. He caresses my skin, worships and cherishes me, kisses and holds me—proves to me how he only knows how to show what's in his heart through actions. If either of us had the words, we might be able to save this...but his mind is made up. He's putting everyone else first, just like he always does, and because I'm an extension of his heart, I come last with him.

It's not fair, but I'm only seeing it from my side. I can't fight against his family. I won't—it's the one thing he has in his life that isn't tainted by mainstream media.

He rolls on a condom and pushes himself into me as I lie on my back. Tears run down my face, wetting the pillow and my ears, but I keep my eyes focused on his in the shadows of his bedroom as he moves slowly in and out of me, so agonizingly slowly and yet too fast because once we both release, it'll all be over.

And then *we* will be over.

His tears drip onto my chest, my cheek, down my lips as he rocks sensually into me. We're both quiet as our bodies connect and souls entwine. There's no moaning and groaning our way through this, just the occasional grunt here or a quiet sniffle there.

I memorize the full feeling of him inside me. I fight away the impending orgasm because I don't want it to happen. He holds his off, too—I see it in the way his lips twist, the way his eyes squeeze shut, the way he pulls out for a beat before he pushes back in. I feel it in the way he holds still inside of me, his eyes intense and loving on mine.

Everything aches except the parts of me he's touching, and I don't know how I'll move forward from this, how I'll ever get past him or find love or happiness again if I can't have it with him. I won't. I know I won't.

When his thrusts turn from slow and tender to a little rougher, a little harder, I know we're both getting close. The intense pleasure is too good to push away, and while neither of us wants this to end, it has to.

Everything ends.

It's a depressing and sad truth, and this time in his bed is just another reminder of that.

I cry through my release, the sobs attacking me as pleasure racks my body. He whispers my name over and over, a prayer on his tongue as he comes.

He collapses over me for a few blissful and quiet moments. I stroke his head where it lays on my chest between my breasts, breathing in his scent and trying to feel and experience every detail. The sandalwood in my nostrils, the softness of his hair beneath my fingertips, the sounds of our heavy breathing mixed with occasional sniffles, the taste of his peppermint mouth, his silhouette in the darkness through my tears.

He gets rid of the condom, and by the time he comes back, I'm already dressed, clutching my plane ticket in my hands.

"Stay," he whispers. "Stay until your flight."

"It's only prolonging the inevitable. If this is the end, I need a clean break."

He pulls on his jeans. "I wish it could be different."

"It could be," I say, my voice full of all the hope that's in my chest.

He walks over toward me and shakes his head sadly. "No, it can't."

I run my fingertips along his jawline then tip my chin up to press a soft kiss to his lips. "Goodbye, Mark."

I don't wait to hear his whispered goodbye. The idea of his last words to me being goodbye is too heavy. I walk out of his bedroom, through his condo, out his front door, and out of his life.

five

I should've stayed at Mark's place, but I had to get out of there. Instead, I spend the next several hours on a hard chair at the airport as I wait for my flight. I board and slide into a seat in first class, thankful for his final gift to me.

I debate texting Jill before we take off to ask if she can pick me up from the airport in a few hours, but I don't want to bother her at four in the morning when my flight lands. I'll catch a cab or get an Uber home. These are the things I allow to occupy my thoughts, because if I allow Mark in my head for even a second, I'll break. Instead, I stare out the window and focus on the darkness the entire flight home.

The house is quiet when I step through the doors, but it's exactly as I left it.

I'm different, though.

The last time I left here, I had a duffel bag—which is still at Mark's house in Los Angeles—and my purse. I still have my purse, but now I have a new duffel filled with things someone else bought for me. Oh, and there's the whole thing with my heart.

I left it on a rooftop in Chicago.

It's weird walking around without that piece of me. I can still breathe, though, and where there's breath, there's hope.

At least that's what I tell myself, because if I wallow in the misery that's ready to crash into me at any second, I'm not sure how I'll survive.

The house is empty. I assume Jill is at Becker's. I take advantage of the peace. I don't think about what just happened; instead, I shut off my thoughts, crawl into bed, close my eyes, and drift to sleep.

When I wake up a few hours later, I finally text Jill.

Me: *I'm back home. Might head to Phoenix for a few days before school starts.*

My phone rings a few minutes later, and I see my best friend's name flash across the screen.

"Hey," I answer.

"What are you doing home? Is Mark with you?"

"Nope." I don't say more. I can't seem to speak around the sudden lump in my throat.

"I'm on my way to an event I have to cover, but then I'll be home and we'll talk, okay?" Her voice is comforting.

I clear my throat and take a sip of water to force that lump away. "Don't worry about me." I don't want to interrupt her life with my bullshit issues.

"Where's Mark?"

"Chicago."

"Why?"

"It's over." Someday I'll be able to say those words without feeling the pain slicing through me.

"Oh my God, Reese! Why? What happened?"

"Their grandfather died, Brian was using me the whole time, Mark beat the shit out of Brian, and then he chose his family over me. Over us."

"Jesus Christ. Okay, this event can wait. I'm on my way home."

"Stop it. You have work to do. I'll be okay."

She sighs. "Give me an hour. Two tops. I'll be there."

"Okay." I'd fight her, but for one thing, it would be futile, and for another, I could use my best friend right now.

My phone notifies me of a text after we hang up. My heart races when I see the name on the screen. I quickly open it to read what he has to say.

Mark: *You make it home ok? I sent a ride to the airport and he said he never found you.*

Me: *I'm home. Got an Uber.*

And that's it. We leave it at that, the last words we'll ever exchange.

That thought is what finally pushes me over the delicate edge I've been balancing on since I left Chicago. I crawl into my bed and allow the grief to wash over me.

I realize I need to get out of bed, need to find something more productive to do with my time. I log onto my laptop and finally check the work email that's been sitting untouched for nearly a month. I have a new one from my principal asking me when I can meet with him. I'm reminded of something Brian said up on that rooftop.

I had to do some handiwork with the principal of her school to make sure Reese would be the one who came begging for a donation.

Did Mr. Monroe know something about FDB Tech Corp? Was he in cahoots with Brian—or was this something Brian did all on his own?

Brian easily could've looked me up. He had half my belongings in his hands when I dumped my purse all over the floor that morning I got off the elevator and ran into him. He could've seen my name or my school keychain or my identification badge—anything, really.

After I clean up my email and write Mr. Monroe back that I'll stop by his office sometime this week, I open last year's syllabus and set to work on revising it. I'm in a foul mood and I'm sure it's leaking through to my bitchy new class policies. I blare some music to distract myself.

Just as I finish the paragraph I'm typing, a Vail song comes on my playlist. I read over my paragraph and delete the whole thing. *No late assignments will be accepted.*

I pull up Lizzie's contact info and shoot off the text I've been thinking about sending all morning to her.

Me: *I hope everyone is doing okay this morning. I'm sorry I had to leave.*

I can only imagine how much Diane will disapprove of me now. Ditching her ailing son a few days before his grandfather's funeral? I'll certainly make her black list now. I wonder if they'll tell her why Brian has a broken face. I wonder if Mark will admit to it. I wonder if Paul will force his boys together in the same room to talk about their issues.

Not that it matters. I'm not planning to be in the lives of any Fox family member beyond these final words to Lizzie.

Lizzie: *I understand. Wish you were here.*

Me: *Me too, but someone bought me a plane ticket out of Chicago.*

Lizzie: *He told me. I hope you and I can still be friends.*

Me: *I'd like that.*

It's a lie. I want out of the Fox family. Lizzie is too much a reminder of what happened, and I don't think being friends with her is a good idea.

Lizzie: *My bachelorette party is in Vegas next month. I can't wait to see you there.*

Me: *Sounds fun.*

It's another lie. I don't want to see her, don't want the reminder of everything I just lost.

Jill comes home a little before lunchtime. She steps tentatively into the family room. "How're you feeling?" she asks.

I'm sprawled on the couch with my laptop as I finalize my lesson plans for the first week. "Not great."

"You want to talk about it?" She plops onto the loveseat perpendicular to the couch.

I lift a shoulder.

"What happened?"

"Mark and I were talking on the roof. He kept pushing me toward Brian. Lizzie says it's because he's so scared he's going to screw it up and hurt me that he'd rather end it now than ruin it later."

Jill rolls her eyes. "That's stupid."

I rehash the whole story again, ending with, "I went to the airport, got on the plane, and came home."

"You're an idiot." She stands up and heads to the refrigerator.

"Excuse me?" My hand flies to my chest as I protect my heart in defense of her words.

"I called you an idiot," she says from the kitchen. She returns a minute later with a banana and collapses back onto the loveseat.

"Why?"

"Because you left. You came home when he loves you. When he needs you."

"He handed me a plane ticket home and told me love wasn't enough." I rub my forehead. "What was I supposed to do?"

"You're supposed to stay and fight for him." She takes a bite of her banana.

"And *you're* supposed to be on my side."

"I *am* on your side, Reese. That's why I'm telling it to you straight." She takes another bite of her banana.

"We all just need a fresh start. I need to be away from them both so they can heal their relationship without me. Especially with the funeral. Mark's life is enough of a circus. They don't need me there as a distraction."

She points her banana in my direction. "That sounds exactly like something Mark would say."

"You don't even know him."

"You're making excuses and letting him end things now instead of ruining it later. But he loves you, and you should always fight for love."

Her words hit their mark. She's not wrong, but I'm too stubborn and bruised right now to admit it.

six

Mark is a steady stream in my thoughts as I concentrate on the deserted road ahead of me. Brian dips his way in and out. A Vail song crashes into my thoughts as I drive. It's one of my old favorites, a song off their first album. I don't belt out the words like I always do. Instead, I listen to the emotion in Mark's voice. His songs are one of the few places where I can see him stripped raw. He allowed me to see that side of him, but he took it away as quickly as he gave it. That's my one biggest regret in this whole thing—that we didn't get more time together, that we only shared a few days that showed me everything we could've had.

I pull into my parents' driveway a little before dinnertime after five long hours in the car. I sit in the car for a second and let the memories of the last time I was in this driveway wash over me. Mark showed up and I sat in the car with him for five hours as we returned to Vegas. Thinking back, that was basically the fuse that lit the rest of the fireworks that ensued.

As soon as my mom pulls me into a hug, the waterworks start. I can't help it. Mom's comforting arms always make me emotional, and after the hell I've been through over the past week, I needed her love. I'm at my breaking point, and time away seems like the only thing that will heal the open wounds.

"What's wrong?" she asks, her voice soothing. "Is it the boy?"

I draw in a shaky breath and pull out of her hug. I nod, swiping away the tears.

"Are you ready to talk about him yet?"

I think I should at this point. I didn't come all this way to shut myself in my childhood bedroom.

She ushers me in. My dad's head pops around the corner. He sees the tears, gives me a hello hug, and makes himself scarce. After years of raising two daughters, he'll be the first to admit that tears are mom's department in this house.

We plop onto the couch and I tell her everything. Well...almost everything.

I tell her how I thought I was in love with one man but started dating someone else before I was ready, fell in love with him as well, then found out they were brothers. I tell her about my trip to Los Angeles with Mark and the emergency trip to Chicago we made. I don't give too many details, but I do mention how one of them is a celebrity, and she freaks out on me.

"Which one? The original one or the brother?" She's squealing, and it's only now I remember why I tend to keep my personal life private. "Who is it? Who? Who?"

I roll my eyes. "You're losing sight of the point."

Her eyes are all alight with excitement, and I realize this is exactly where I learned my habits of reading gossip magazines and watching entertainment news programs.

"You're right. I'm sorry." I can see in her eyes she's itching to know, and I'm frankly shocked my sister hasn't already told her.

"Rachel didn't mention any of this to you?" I ask.

Her eyes widen. "Rachel knows? That little brat!"

I roll my eyes. As annoying as this entire conversation is, it still feels good to be talking to my mom and getting some of the pain off my chest.

"Again, missing the point."

"Right. Sorry." She nods and salutes me.

"Anyway, it turns out Brian was just using me to get back at his brother. They're competitive when it comes to women, and I guess Mark told him he had feelings for me."

"Brian...Brian Hutchinson?" she asks hopefully, naming one of her favorite soap opera stars.

I roll my eyes. "No."

"Brian Williams?"

I shake my head. "It's not Brian anybody, and you're missing the point again."

"Right. So it's Mark, then? Hmm..." She taps her finger on her chin thoughtfully. "Mark the Shark?"

My brows furrow.

"The host of that fish show on Animal Planet. He's cute."

"Ew, Mom. No."

"Mark...give me a hint. Is he an actor?"

I heave out an exasperated breath. "It's Mark Ashton."

She knows what this means. She heard the teenaged Reese talk obsessively about him with teenaged Jill. My dad took us to our first Vail concert.

Her cheeks grow pink—another trait I got from her—and her eyes nearly pop out of her head. "The cute singer you had that poster of hanging on your wall?"

I nod as I think of the poster that used to hang in my bedroom, a twenty-something heartthrob in ripped jeans and no shirt.

"The one from that reality show that was on a few years ago?"

"One and the same."

"The one who is a known ladies' man?" She asks that one a little softer in the event my dad is listening.

"It's all an image his publicist paints." I don't mention the fact that he *has* slept with an awful lot of women and *some* of what we see is probably true.

"And you love him?"

I sigh. "I do."

"And he loves you?"

I nod.

Her brows draw down sharply. "Then why aren't you with him?"

"It's complicated. He's putting his family first and I'm respecting his wishes. Isn't that what you do when you love someone?"

She shakes her head. "No, baby girl. When you love someone, you fight for them."

* * *

The next day, we go shopping, Mom's cure for everything from a common cold to heartbreak, but it doesn't lessen the sting. Sleeping in my childhood home feels good, but I know this won't last long.

The following day, I'm scrolling the home page on my mom's laptop when I come across the headline in entertainment news. *Vail Front Man Mark Ashton Attends Grandfather's Funeral.*

I abuse myself further by clicking the video accompanying the article.

The video begins with a wide angle shot of a large group of people walking toward the cameras through the green grass of a cemetery on a sunny day. My eyes find Mark. An array of yelling voices bursts into the shot, and I jump in the chair and scramble to turn down the volume. "Are the rumors true that you've fallen in love?" "Who died?" "Is she here?" "What about the woman you were spotted kissing at Sevens?" "Will you and Ethan be hitting the town tonight?"

He doesn't address the paparazzi, simply keeps his head down. I see Brian with his arm around Diane. Paul's on her other side. Lizzie and Dave walk a few paces behind them. In the background, I can make out Ethan, Steve, and James. Angelique and Morgan are there, too. Becker and Jill walk beside Jason. The video zooms steadily onto Mark. His grandmother's arm is looped through his, and my heart twists. I should be there with him. I should be holding his hand, walking beside him, helping him through his grandfather's funeral.

I watch as Vinny rushes toward the camera with his arms spread open as if to shield Mark from the photographers. "It's a funeral, people," he yells, his image looming larger in the camera's field while Mark is blocked from view. "Have a little respect." The video ends there.

Now I get it. Now I understand what Mark hates most about his job. He told me he doesn't have any privacy, and he's right. He told me the media paints a picture of him, and I wonder how they'll twist the sweet images of him holding onto his grandmother at her husband's funeral to turn him back into the rock star sex god everyone knows him as.

A burning rage fills my veins for him. I'm guilty—I'm one of the very people who has spent her time looking for these types of pictures. Oh, a private wedding on an island and there's an exclusive photo in that magazine? Awesome. Oh, a picture of that celebrity supercouple's first baby? Let me see. Oh, a rare photo of Mark Ashton holding his grandmother's hand? Let me cut that one out for the scrapbook.

I'm disgusted with these people, but I'm ashamed of myself for spending so much time buying into it. This video and the accompanying photos tell the general public nothing about this man. They don't know how kind he is, or how funny, or how he puts everyone else first. They don't know the battles he wages inside. They don't know how he bottles his emotions and blows them out into his music or into a quiet embrace on a rooftop. They don't know he almost died once because of an overdose. They don't know about the couch on his roof or the buildings that inspired his lyrics. These are the private things he allowed me to see—the things some gossip rag would never print because that's not the rock star image his publicist paints of him.

I close my browser and stare at the blank screen for a few beats as I allow myself to really *feel*. I love him. I love him so much it physically hurts.

I pull out my phone and open the last message from him. I stare at the screen, debating what to say. I want to tell him I'm sorry about his grandfather's funeral and for the paparazzi being there and for me not being there. I want to say how much I love him and what a big mistake I made taking that ticket out of town and away from him, how my heart aches without him and how I can barely function. How much I miss him and need him. I start to type all the words.

He's the one who wanted this, not me.

Clean break, I remind myself. It's the only possible way I'll ever be able to get over him.

I select all my text and delete it before I do something I can't take back. I text Lizzie for Gram's address, and once she texts back, I send a bouquet of flowers and a note expressing my condolences.

It's not enough. I wish I could be there, but now it's time to live with the consequences of my actions.

* * *

"We have some news," Rachel says. She and Ben are standing in front of my parents' mantle, the place where we took pictures on Christmas morning as kids—even though I always wondered what the hell we needed a fireplace for in the middle of the desert. Santa Claus, I suppose, and photo opportunities.

I can guess what her news is from the glow in her eyes and the way she's not so inconspicuously hiding her left hand behind Ben.

We all knew this was coming eventually, and I'm thrilled for my little sister.

But it's also a stark reminder that I've had three failed relationships in the last year, each one progressively more heartbreaking than the last.

My mom's cheeks burn pink with excitement as she waits for Rachel to spill the beans.

"We're getting married!" she finally says, pulling her arm out from behind Ben's back. She holds her hand out toward us, showing off the sparkly new diamond on her finger.

I push down the jealousy that runs through my chest and pop up from the couch. I hug my future brother-in-law first since my sister is attacked by our mother. I go through the motions, painting on a face of happiness for my sister. She deserves this—deserves to have her sister present in this moment, happy and excited for her.

When I hug Rachel, she says, "I want you to be my maid of honor."

"Of course," I say. "I'd be honored."

My dad pops a bottle of champagne and my mom asks about ten thousand questions and all I can think of is Mark's tears dripping onto my chest when we made love before I left Chicago.

"Have you thought about a date yet?" my mom asks Rachel.

"This just happened a few hours ago, so I haven't thought about anything. But I want a long engagement. We've both got so much going on at work right now that we're either eloping tomorrow or we're planning a huge wedding in a couple years."

"A couple years?" my mom screeches. "But what about grandbabies? Do I have to wait a couple years for grandbabies?"

Rachel looks at me and rolls her eyes, and I can't help the giggle that bubbles out of me. It feels good to laugh with family—to *be* with family, to be somewhere I know I belong, a place where people want me to be here and don't say goodbye by sending me out of town with a plane ticket.

The more I think about it, the more pissed off I become about everything—the unexplained woman at Sevens, the way Mark pushed me toward his brother, how he ended it with me over the phone while I stood in a bathroom stall at the hospital. Kicking me out before the funeral and sending me home.

What an asshole.

I drink champagne to forget about him. I ward off the tears I feel pressing hotly against my eyelids, playing them off as happy tears for my sister.

I want to talk to Rachel about everything that happened with Brian and Mark, and I will. Tonight just isn't that night. Tonight's for celebrating.

I head home the next day without a chance to dissect my life with my sister. I need to get ready for school, and as good as it felt to be home with family, I need to start picking up the pieces of my life and moving in a forward direction.

When I get home from the five-hour drive from my parents' house, I check my phone. I have a new Snapchat from Jill. I click it and chuckle as I look at a picture of her lunch. Without thinking, I swipe over to the page with my friends' stories.

The problem? I never unfollowed Mark's account.

A new story from Mark Ashton posted just a little while ago sits waiting for me. He didn't send it directly to me. He posted it to his story for the whole world to see.

I realize he can click one button to see who has viewed his story and my name will be among those who have, but I can't stop myself. I tap his name and his face fills my screen.

But it's not just *his* face.

There are no words, no filters, no doodles to accompany the image. Just Mark, eyes glassy and looking like he's had a lot to drink, with his cheek against some other woman's cheek. I've never seen her before. She looks nothing like me, but she's gorgeous with her straight copper hair, dark eyes, and eyelashes I can practically grab through my screen they're so long. She has glassy eyes like Mark and the same sort of haze only drunk people wear.

I'd like to pretend this is one of those older pictures his publicist posted for the world to see, but that's not how Snapchat works. He took this picture with this woman today.

All I see are the faces of two people looking too cozy. For seven short seconds, the image claws at my soul. I don't replay it—I'm not masochistic, but I consider it for a few seconds. I don't need to see it again. The image is burned into my mind and will stay with me for a long time to come. But I still can't bring myself to unfollow his account.

seven

"I have something I need to talk to you about." Jill sounds nervous as she sits next to me on the couch the next morning before she goes to work, and a pang of anxiety darts through my chest.

"What?"

"Our lease is up for renewal on October first."

I nod. The date is marked in my calendar, but now that I know for sure I'm not moving in with Brian, I just assumed we'd let the renewal happen like we've done for the past three years.

She clears her throat. "We have to give thirty days' notice if we plan to move."

My brows draw in.

"I...um—it's just..." She draws in a breath then blurts out the words. "Becker asked me to move in with him."

My jaw drops a bit. "He did?"

She nods. She looks so nervous to tell me that I can't help but lean over to give her an awkward couch hug. "I'm so happy for you."

"But what about you?"

I lift a shoulder, masking the fact that the same thought is running through my head. I'll have to give up what seems to be the one good thing I have going for me—sharing a house I love with my best friend. There's no way I can afford the rent on this place by myself, and I don't want to live alone. I've never lived alone. Jill has been my roommate since I moved out of my parents' house.

I shake my head. Jill doesn't need to worry about it. She just needs to know she has her best friend's support. "I'll figure something out."

Maybe I should just move back to Phoenix. I'd consider the option if I wasn't tied into a contract and about to start a new school year in a few days. I think of Tess next. I wonder if she'd let me crash in her guest room for a while, or we could get a new place together.

After my conversation with Jill, I decide sitting around wondering what to do won't get me anywhere. In an effort to utilize my energy for something good, I go to school. I check in with the secretary and get my keys. I pop my head into my principal's office, but he's in a meeting with another teacher. I'll try again before I go home.

I head to my classroom, and it looks just like I left it in May but with cleaner carpets. Desks are stacked against one wall, and I start the tedious and sweaty process of unstacking them and putting them into a new seating arrangement. We'll start the year in pods of four and see where it takes us.

This all feels so meaningless, the workout of moving desks and chairs, wiping down my white boards, logging onto my computer. I go through the motions, but I have no emotional ties to any of it. I write up goals and the date for the first day of school and organize my desk drawers. I print my syllabus. It's all shit I can do next week with the inevitable time we'll get in our classrooms, but now it's done.

I decide to start the copies of my six-paged syllabus in the copy room before I head back to Mr. Monroe's office.

When I walk in, I see the one person I was hoping not to run into today.

His brows shoot up when he sees me. He's wearing khaki shorts and a black Desert Lights High School shirt and he holds a piece of paper in his hands. His light brown hair is shorter than it used to be, and his eyes seem like a richer shade of dark chocolate than I remember. "Reese Brady," he says, his lips tipping up in a smile.

"Justin Nolan," I say, mimicking his tone.

It's funny how less than a year ago, this was the guy I thought I was going to marry someday. Looking at him now after everything I've been through in the past few months, I can honestly say I don't feel a thing for him anymore.

My parents loved him, he fit in well with my sister and Ben, and I saw a happy future with him. It was the very second things started getting serious that he wanted out. He wasn't ready for marriage and kids, and nothing proved that more than the day he broke my heart by throwing the opposite of the old cliché at me. It wasn't *him*, it was *me*.

He just didn't see me as his wife.

It was a sad reality I finally moved on from, and now here he stands in the copy room. I managed to avoid him except at faculty meetings the last half of last year. It was easy since he's in the science department and I teach English.

"How was your summer?" he asks.

I can't help my grimace as I reflect on Reese's Summer of Sin in Sin City. "Eventful. Yours?"

He nods. "It was good." He looks down at the sheet of paper in his hands and I step over to one of the open copiers. I punch the numbers I need into the machine and start the job.

It's a little awkward standing in silence in a room containing only my ex and me, but he breaks the silence with small talk.

"What sort of events filled your summer?"

I debate how much to tell him. "I started seeing someone." I'm not sure why those are the words that slip out. Maybe to be hurtful, or maybe to just let him know I've moved on.

He smiles. "Good. I'm happy for you."

"I'm not seeing him anymore." I watch as the pages flip out of the machine into the tray.

"Oh."

"I traveled a little. Phoenix, Los Angeles, Chicago." I leave it at that. He doesn't need to know who I was with or why I went.

He sets some more papers in the copier he stands in front of and punches in some numbers. "How are the Bradys?"

"They're good. My sister's the same, still with Ben. They just got engaged. How's your family?" It's weird to be making small talk with someone I was about to make a lifelong commitment to just eight months ago, but at this point I can hardly remember our time together.

"Good. My sister started dating some guy from New York."

"New York? How did that happen?"

"He threw out a bunch of money at her table one night and they got to talking. He only played at her table because he was attracted to her." She's a blackjack dealer downtown.

I chuckle. "And she fell for that?"

"She fell for him, I guess."

"What did you do all summer?" I ask.

He lifts a shoulder. "I had science camp with the kids. Spent some time volunteering, building houses with Habitat for Humanity."

"Ugh," I mutter as I think about what a truly good guy he is. We could've had it all, but he chose to end it and now I'm not even a little bit in that place anymore.

Instead, I find myself hung up on an unattainable rock star like some obsessed teenager who needs to get a life.

Seeing Justin sparks a new fire in me. I want to move forward—not with a man, but I want to gain my own footing back.

Who knew all it would take is a heart shattered by a pair of brothers to find some closure with my ex?

"You want to grab a drink?" Justin asks. My head whips up from watching the monotonous papers roll out of the machine, newly decorated with the black ink from the words I typed.

"Oh, I don't think so. But thanks for offering."

He doesn't do a very good job hiding the fact that he's offended by my rejection.

"I'm just not in a place to grab a drink with an ex right now," I say.

Understanding lights his eyes. "I didn't mean like that," he says. "I'm...uh—I've met someone."

"You've met someone?" I ask. In the past, the fact that he'd moved on might've hurt me. But hearing it now doesn't have that effect on me.

He nods. "At science camp, of all places."

I chuckle. He's pretty hot for a science nerd. "I'm happy for you, Justin."

"Thanks. I only asked because you seem like you could use a friend."

"What makes you say that?" I ask.

"The way you're staring at those copies like you want them to hurry up so you can run the hell out of here. The way you've heaved out enough carbon dioxide to make a can of soda."

My brows furrow.

"Carbon dioxide is what we breathe out, and it's also used in carbonated beverages," he says, as if he just clarified his earlier statement.

My brows draw down further.

"You're exhaling a lot," he says, pulling his papers from his copy machine. He gathers up the other papers he copied and steps closer to me. "Sighing. I've never seen you like this, and you might recall my soft shoulder and open ear and all that if you need someone to talk to."

He's inviting me to spill my guts using the words he always said to me when I was having a bad day.

"Thanks, Justin. I appreciate it. I'll be okay."

"What happened to you, Reese?" he asks softly.

"I had my heart broken."

He touches my shoulder in a friendly gesture. "You became my best friend when we were together, and I miss that. I miss our friendship. I miss *you*." I keep my eyes focused on the copy machine. "The only reason I ended things was because you started feeling more like a friend to me than a girlfriend. But that feeling of love—friend or otherwise—it doesn't just disappear overnight."

I nod, refusing to move my focus from my papers, refusing to let the heat burning behind my eyes turn into tears. "Thanks," I whisper, and then he leaves.

My copies finish running and I head for Mr. Monroe's office. "Come on in," he says when I knock on the doorframe.

"You wanted to see me?" I want to ask about his connection to Brian, but I'm not sure how to work it into the conversation.

"Yes. Have a seat." He clicks a few buttons on his computer then faces me. I study him for a few beats. William Monroe is in his sixties, I think, and he has grey hair and wears glasses and a suit to work every day. He's shrewd and smart, and I feel a little like I'm in trouble as I sit in the principal's office.

"Ms. Brady, the senior English team needs a new direction, and I'd like you to be the lead."

"What about Devin?" I ask, naming last year's lead.

"He won't be returning this year."

"He won't?" I'm stunned. Devin had the kind of school spirit and excitement for teaching everyone in the profession should have. I want to ask what happened, but I refrain. I'm sure I'll hear it through the grapevine eventually, but I'm surprised I've fallen so far out of the loop.

He shakes his head but doesn't offer further details. "The level lead comes with compensation and extra responsibility. Is that something you'd be up for?"

I know what it entails—extra meetings, organizing a team of around ten teachers, and keeping everyone on the same page so all our students are offered a similar challenge regardless of who their teacher is.

Extra responsibility sounds like the perfect focus for me. It'll give me something to throw my energy into. "I'd love to," I say.

"Great. Theresa will email you some paperwork and you can get started next week. Kathryn will be in touch with your responsibilities."

"Thank you for thinking of me," I say. I get up to leave.

"One last thing, Ms. Brady."

I turn back around to face him.

"Thank you for your work with FDB Tech Corp. Their generous donation will go far this year."

This is my chance, so I grab it. "About that, Mr. Monroe. Did the president of that company ever get in touch with you?"

Mr. Monroe nods. "Mr. Fox called me in May to inquire about our Homecoming donations. He mentioned he saw on the website how we have our teachers work with local businesses, and he specifically requested you."

"And that was it?"

Mr. Monroe nods. "Was there something else?" he asks.

I shake my head, glad it's cleared up as I go into this school year—glad Mr. Monroe is none the wiser about what went down with the Fox brothers. Those personal details are things my boss never needs to know about my life. "Thank you."

I text Tess as I slide into the driver's seat of my car.

Me: *Are you free for dinner?*

She doesn't reply until I'm home twenty minutes later.

Tess: *Just ate, but I'm free for drinks. I can sit with you while you eat.*

Me: *You want to come over?*

Tess: *Sure, be there in an hour.*

When my doorbell rings a half hour later, I assume it's Tess a little early.

I'm wrong.

Brian Fox stands on my porch. He's wearing a suit and a gash still stretches across the bridge of his nose, though it looks a lot better than it did a few days ago. Bruises shadow his eyes, but they're not as black as I would've imagined after the beating he took. He looks like my dick of an ex-boyfriend, but despite that, he still looks like the hot business mogul he is.

"What are you doing here?" I ask.

"Can we talk?"

"Go ahead," I say, gripping the door with one hand and not inviting him in.

He clears his throat. "Can I come in?"

"No." I shake my head and press my lips together.

He blows out a sigh. "I came here to tell you how sorry I am. I said some pretty awful things, and you didn't deserve that. I was hurting and I was drunk. When I drink too much, I lash out. I say things I don't mean, things that aren't true."

"Are you really standing on my porch telling me that you weren't using me to get back at him?"

He shakes his head. "I won't deny that's how it started for me. But I didn't expect to fall in love with you along the way."

I roll my eyes.

"It's the truth."

"What do you want?" I ask.

"I want to apologize."

"For saying the things you said or for getting caught?"

"For coming between you and him. For the intentions I had when I started something with you. But I'm not sorry for falling in love with you."

My heart softens just the tiniest bit, but I'm too hurt by the fact that he only ever wanted to be with me in the first place as an act of revenge.

So instead of accepting his apology, I think about the things he said. Regardless of whether or not they were true, they were still hurtful, and with that in mind, I lash out at him. "I never wanted you half as much as I want your brother."

I go to close the door, but his parting words freeze me in place.

"Then why aren't you with him?" His voice is soft.

I open the door to stare at him with my jaw hanging open. "Because of you!"

"I want to make it up to you."

"You came between me and what could have been the love of my life. How do you think you can make it up to me?"

He lifts an unsure shoulder. "I don't have an answer for you. But I do have these." He reaches into his pocket and pulls something out into a closed fist. He holds his fist out to me, and I open my hand.

He drops two orange chips that read *Cosmopolitan* into my palm.

Pumpkins.

Two of them.

That's two thousand dollars sitting in the literal palm of my hand.

"They were always yours," he says softly. "I'm sorry for everything I did. I'm sorry for coming between you and Mark. I'm sorry I fell in love with you along the way. But most of all, I'm sorry for saying things that hurt you." He turns and walks to his car, and I stare at the pumpkins in my palm in stunned silence as he gets in his car and drives away.

He didn't wait around for me to accept his apology or thank him for the chips or throw them in his face. I wouldn't have done any of those things.

He didn't even wait around for me to say that he's a liar. He never fell in love with me, because if he did, he would've been strong enough to let me go the very moment he realized my heart belonged with his brother.

eight

When my bell rings a half hour later, this time it really is Tess. She comes bearing a bottle of vodka and a huge purse that looks stuffed full. I raise an eyebrow at the purse as I invite her in.

"I read into the tone of your text and figured this was going to be a drinking night, so I brought an overnight bag just in case." She sashays past me and drops her bag on the floor. "Drink first or talk first?"

I nod toward the vodka. "That just seems like a ridiculous question."

She laughs and twists the top off the bottle, takes a swig, and passes it to me. I take a shot, too.

"What's going on?" she asks.

"The short version is Brian and I are done. Oh, and I slept with Mark Ashton again and he's in love with me but love isn't enough."

She stares at me for a few long beats without speaking. She doesn't even blink as she tilts her head. "Wait...what?"

I nod to my couch and we both head that direction. She brings the bottle with her, and as we pass it back and forth, I spill the entire sordid story from start to finish, including the fact that Brian just stopped by here with an apology I never accepted.

I don't mention the pumpkins, and I'm not sure why. I guess it sort of feels like payment for all the sex, which it isn't, but I'm also not giving it back. Two thousand dollars is a lot of money for someone like me.

I take another sip of vodka. "Mark isn't ready for a real relationship. And then he had this snap with another girl."

No matter how much I try to believe the photos that appear on his social media accounts almost every night are from the pre-Reese days, I can't help but believe *some* of the women he's been with have to be more recent. Wouldn't someone somewhere along the way say something if they were all old photos? Wouldn't someone find some new photos to post to prove he wasn't wherever Penny says he was?

Did Penny release those photos of him the night he went to Sevens when I was in Chicago?

I can't help but wonder if someone else's hidden agenda was at play...namely, Brian's. I clearly remember him talking quietly in a hallway while I got ready for bed. Is it possible he was setting us up?

"Snap?" Tess's voice pulls me out of my thoughts.

"Snapchat. He snapped a picture of him with some girl and sent it to everyone in the world. He's already moving on."

She takes the bottle from my hand. "Dick move. How did the snap make you feel?"

I pause and let her question sink in. I let myself really feel for a second, and only one word comes to mind. "Devastated."

The word hangs between us for a beat, and then I change the subject. "How have you been? Are you still seeing Jason?"

"On and off. He bought a house not too far from Beck's new place."

"Things are going good?" I ask.

She shrugs. "Things are going."

"Not good?"

"I like him," she says. "And I'm pretty sure one of us will fuck it up."

Her words remind me a lot of Mark's reason for running away from me.

"How?"

"I'm not cut out for a relationship. I'll sleep with someone else and pretend it was because we haven't labeled anything yet or I'll push him away or I'll do something stupid."

"Maybe you just haven't met the right person yet." I say the words softly to lessen their blow.

She lifts a shoulder and she won't meet my gaze. "Maybe not." She blows out a breath. She isn't one to allow people to see her vulnerable side. She can talk about sex all day, but when it comes to emotions, she gets uncomfortable.

It isn't until the next morning that I bring up the whole reason I asked Tess over in the first place.

We both fell asleep on my couch watching a marathon of romantic comedy movies, and I wake up with a stiff neck and a headache from too much vodka.

As soon as I stand up, Tess jerks awake. "Fuck," she mutters as she rolls her neck.

"What?"

"My neck hurts."

"Have Jason massage it out," I mumble.

She rolls her eyes. "Let a girl wake up before you start in on that shit again."

"You could've slept in the guest room."

"You could've slept in your own room," she shoots back.

"Fair enough. Speaking of which, I have a favor to ask. It's actually why I invited you over last night." I stand up and use both of my hands to attempt some self-shoulder massaging.

She raises a brow then leans her head back against the couch. "What?"

"Can I crash with you a while?"

"Sure. Why?"

"Jill's moving in with Becker and our lease is up."

"Of course." She sits up a little straighter. "My guest room is yours. My place is small, but we'll make it work."

"Thanks." I head toward the kitchen to get some coffee going.

She stands and stretches. "I should get going." She disappears down my hallway, presumably to use the bathroom. I'm glad to have a place to live, but I'm already wondering how this will change the dynamic between us.

* * *

I spend the weekend packing boxes. Jill let our rental company know we won't be renewing our lease, and they offered us our full deposit back if we move out a month early. We jumped at the chance, so I only have a couple weeks to get packed and moved just as a new school year begins.

It's Sunday night, the night before teachers go back to school, when the doorbell rings. I'm in the middle of pulling everything out of our kitchen cabinets and the place is a disaster—as am I. The counters are filled with cups and bowls and plates as I put Jill's things on one side of the kitchen and mine on the other. I'm not expecting anybody, and I'm surprised when I open the door to find my ex-boyfriend standing there.

"What are you doing here?" I ask, opening the door and motioning for Justin to come in.

"Tradition," Justin says. He hands me a binder. "It's your turn."

I laugh, take the binder from him, and motion him in. He steps into my home—a place where he used to be welcome, where he used to stay all the time like it was a second home to him.

We worked together at DLHS for two years before we started dating, and I remember the first meeting when we started to get to know one another. We were forced to group with teachers from other subject areas, bored stiff at a faculty training as we learned nothing new. He passed me a note, and I wrote back. Then we started coming up with actual methods for critical thinking we could both use in our classes, and a few weeks later, I put all our ideas in a binder and had a student drop it off in his classroom. Over the years, we both added new ideas to it—things any teacher could use in any classroom, regardless of the subject matter. We'd add silly notes or doodles, too, and we'd send someone over to deliver it. It became tradition to drop it off at the other's house the night before we returned to school, filled with all sorts of ideas we came up with over the summer.

And now it's sitting on my counter and I sort of wonder what new content he's added to it.

"What's with the boxes?" He nods toward the wall lined with them.

"I'm moving," I say.

"Why?"

"Jill's moving in with her boyfriend and I'm moving in with Tess."

His brows draw down. "With *Tess*?"

I chuckle. "I forgot how much you never liked her."

"I never said that," he says defensively.

I tilt my head to the side and narrow my eyes at him. "Actually, you did once. You had way too much beer that night, but I distinctly remember you telling me she was loud and obnoxious."

He has the grace to look a little embarrassed. "I said that?"

I nod. "It's a fair assessment, but I love her anyway." I get back to work in the kitchen as I sort through a bunch of shot glasses we don't even use anymore.

"Do you need some help?" he asks.

I lift a shoulder. "If you want to make me some new boxes, I wouldn't say no." I nod over to the tape gun and the flat cardboard. "You want a drink?"

"I'll take a beer if you have one."

I nod and pull out a beer for him and a bottle of water for me. He sets to work on the boxes. We're both quiet for a while as we work. I finally clear my throat and blurt the only thing I can think of. "Tell me about your new girlfriend."

His eyes light up, and he doesn't even need to say a word before I know he's in love with her. She's the lucky girl he'll marry someday. "Her name's Alex and she works at the science center. She's a program specialist."

"She's a science nerd like you?"

He laughs. "Yeah."

"How'd you meet?"

"She organized our entire science summer camp. We'd talk while the kids explored the science center, and I asked her to dinner on the second day."

"Cute."

"We've spent every day together since."

"Sounds pretty serious."

He tapes another box, the loud sound of the tape gun interrupting another beat of quiet between us.

"It is. I'm pretty sure I'm going to marry her." He blows out a breath and looks up at me.

"You are?" I ask. "After a couple months?"

He nods. "Crazy, right? But it just feels different."

I give him a small smile. Sometimes it doesn't take long to fall all the way, and I was just there. "I'm happy for you."

"I'm sorry about how things went down between us."

"It's okay, Justin." I'm not sure I would've said that four or five months ago, but everything is so different now. "I moved on. We both did."

"I'm glad. But can I ask what happened to you?" he asks.

My first inclination is that I don't want to talk about it with my ex. But my second thought is that I could use a friend. When I look at him, I see a lot of good memories, but I don't feel love in the pit of my stomach or the searing heartbreak any longer. I only see a person who cares about me, and I can't see anything wrong with confiding in someone who's just a friend. Some male perspective might help me wade through the hurt swimming in my chest.

My eyes fill with unexpected tears. "You broke my heart. It started to heal, and then I met someone new, and then he and his brother proceeded to shatter it."

Justin drops the box he just taped. "He *and his brother*?"

I nod and keep my focus on the plates on the counter. "It's a long story."

"I'm sorry you were hurt," he says.

I draw in a deep breath. "Thank you."

"And I'm sorry I hurt you first."

I tilt my head as I stare at my ex. He's still handsome. I wouldn't want to be a teenager in his class—I'd be embarrassed I suck at science as much as I do in front of a guy that good looking. But I don't feel that spark, not anymore. All my sparks are reserved for one rock star I can't have. "I'm glad you did."

He looks surprised. "Why?"

"Because if you hadn't, I wouldn't have met Mark."

"Mark?"

"One of the brothers." I leave out the fact that it's Mark *Ashton* we're talking about. After I told my mom, I realized I can't talk about him and have an unbiased conversation when I toss his name around.

"What about the other brother?"

"Brian. He turned out to be someone I never thought he was." I think of the pumpkins sitting in my jewelry box on my dresser. I need to go cash those in, but they also symbolize the fact that it's possible Brian isn't as bad as I've made him out to be in my mind.

"Sounds like an adventurous summer."

"It was, but I'm ready to leave Reese's Summer of Sin behind me."

nine

School starts, which also keeps my mind off my issues...sort of. Mark is always present, always in my mind, his name always the word on the tip of my tongue. I throw myself into lesson plans and my new leadership position as I try unsuccessfully to forget about him and everything I went through this summer.

The Summer of Sin wasn't as fun as I thought it would be. It was more like the Summer of Heartbreak.

A few days into the school year, I find an envelope addressed to me in my mailbox with a return address from Chicago.

I tear it open, and the front of the card simply says *Thanks* in scripted font.

It's from Gram.

The words inside bring every single feeling right back to the surface, and I'm in tears by the time I'm done reading.

Reese,

Thank you for the flowers. Your thoughtfulness is appreciated. I wish you could've been there for the boys, but I understand what happened. Mark confided in me, and I have to tell you, I've never seen him look at a girl the way he looks at you. You hung the sun in his sky. I know there are complications, namely Brian, but take it from someone who recently lost the love of her life. You don't have time to waste. Another second apart from the man you belong with is one more second you don't get to share with each other, and that's a downright shame.

Hugs,

Gram

I tuck the note into the middle of a notebook and shove it in my desk. I can't deal with her words right now. I have a stack of essays to look through and I'm facing forward. Allowing her words to percolate in my mind will only take me back to the past.

* * *

"Oh my God, Billy, put down the glue stick. Are you serious right now?" This is *not* something I should have to say to a damn senior in high school on the second Friday afternoon of the school year as he decorates a girl's entire arm with glue. I barely restrain myself from actually using a curse word.

I hate my job this year. I don't blame the kids, or the school, or my rigorous schedule—really, I don't. If it were any other year, I'd be fine. I'd be loving *Beowulf* and argumentative writing.

I blame Mark.

I haven't stopped thinking about him even though I left Chicago over a month ago. I never refollowed any of his social media, but I also never unfollowed his Snapchat. Even though he proved to me he doesn't post to his own Twitter account, I still pull it up every now and then to torture myself...or to see what's going on in his life—to see how his publicist is portraying him.

Lizzie has kept in touch with me, despite my efforts to distance myself, and we're friends even after what went down with her brothers. She texts me almost every day, usually checking in, sometimes funny memes, sometimes just an emoji. She's been a good friend to me, but I can't say I've been the same to her. I should consider myself lucky she keeps putting forth the effort, but she just reminds me of everything I could've had.

My phone buzzes in my pocket just before lunch with a new text. I have exactly four minutes before the bell is going to ring. I hate waiting, but it's unprofessional to take my phone out to read my texts when I have students sitting in front of me.

I've managed to shut everyone in my life out, including Jill. I'm thrilled she's happy with Becker, and I'm happy she's in love. But seeing her around Becker is a stark reminder of everything I don't have. When she's not home, I blast my favorite Vail songs on repeat. It's masochistic, but it makes me feel like he's with me, and that's the one thing that makes me feel better. I'm moving in with Tess this weekend, and I'm hoping living with someone who's around more often will help.

Billy puts away the glue stick, the bell rings, and I'm released to my half hour of quiet time.

I slide my phone out of my pocket to check my text.

Lizzie: *I'll be in Vegas next weekend for my bachelorette party. I'd love to see you and celebrate with you.*

Seeing her will only drag up all the memories I've been trying to push away. It takes me all of five seconds to invent a lie.

Me: *I'm heading home to Phoenix next weekend. Sorry! Would have been fun. Too bad it's not this weekend.*

Lizzie: *Good, because I lied. It's this weekend and I'm already here in town. You better not flake on me.*

I let out a chuckle despite myself. I have to give the girl credit. She knows me better than I realized.

Me: *What's your plan?*

Lizzie: *We're staying at Cosmopolitan. Cabana today, buffet for dinner, club tonight. Drinking, necklaces with plastic dicks all over them, the whole works.*

Me: *Who is "we"?*

Lizzie: *A handful of my girls. You're one of them.*

Me: *I work until 3:00 today.*

Lizzie: *Can you meet us around eight at the buffet at Cosmo?*

I think of my best friend who I've barely seen lately. This could be the perfect chance for a girls' night out.

Me: *I'll see you then. Can I bring a friend?*

Lizzie: *Bring whoever you want. I can't wait to squeeze you, my friend. XO*

I don't reply, but her simple response brings tears to my eyes. She's my one link to the two men who fucked me up so royally.

* * *

When I walk into the Cosmopolitan with Jill a little before eight, I'm attacked by the memories of the last time I was here. I was with Brian. We gambled, we danced, we almost had public sex, and the entire time, I was thinking about Mark. Funny how much has changed, but one thing still remains the same: Mark is on my mind.

I spot Lizzie right away. She's wearing a short, tight, white dress with sequins all over it, a pink sash declaring her the bride to be, and a veil. Six other women stand behind her. She runs to me and grabs me up in a hug, and that's when I notice the plastic dicks all over her veil.

"Classy veil," I tease, though my heart races as my mouth speaks the homophone for her brother's band. I draw in a sharp breath. I can't help but wonder: Why the Cosmopolitan? Why do we have to be here, of all places, when I have memories here with one brother and memories directly next door with another?

The Mandarin Oriental loomed large beside us as we pulled into the Cosmopolitan. Is Mark here in town tonight? Or is he off living his life, performing for a screaming crowd or recording new songs or charming the panties off women everywhere?

Lizzie pulls back and holds me by my biceps. "How've you been?" she asks, giving me a long once over.

I lift a shoulder. I refuse to cry. I won't cry. Why the hell is one simple question from her making the heat sting behind my eyes? "Been better, been worse."

She nods and presses her lips together. "About the same as him, then."

I brush away a single tear that refused to listen to me.

"Oh, honey." She pulls me back into a hug. "I'm so sorry."

One of her friends tugs her arm. "Let's go get in line."

She gives me another long look. "I'm here through Sunday. We'll find some time to talk, okay?"

I force a smile and nod, then Jill falls into step beside me as we make our way into the restaurant. One of the girls in the group hands Jill and me each necklaces with candy shaped like penises.

"You okay?" Jill whispers as she nudges me.

I nod without looking at her, because I know if I look over at her, I'll just see all the concern in her eyes and then I'll fall apart. I pull the penis necklace over my head and bite off one of the dicks.

Tonight's supposed to be fun, not about tears, hurt, and dredging up the pain of the past.

Jill and I sit at the end of the table. We all get our food in shifts, one of the downsides to eating at a buffet, so there's less chatting. Mostly I talk to Jill because Lizzie is busy with her other friends—friends who traveled from all over the country to celebrate with her in Vegas. I know she's doing her best to talk to everyone, but I'm just glad I brought a friend with me so I wouldn't be the odd one out sitting at the table where I only know the bride.

When Jill excuses herself to the bathroom, though, that sentiment is blown to bits. I stare down at my plate quietly.

"You're Reese?" the girl across the table from me asks.

I look up at her and nod.

"I'm Julie, one of Lizzie's bridesmaids."

"Nice to meet you." I take a sip of water. I didn't get an alcoholic beverage, and I wish I had one in my hand. Well, if I'm wishing for things, I wish I was home in my pajamas. Or if I'm *really* wishing for things, I wish I was in Mark's arms—wherever he is.

"Are you the one who dated both brothers?"

I duck my head in some combination of shame and mortification. "Yeah."

"Julie, stop it!" Lizzie's voice interrupts us.

"I'm just saying she's a lucky girl to land *both*. How many other people can say they've done *that*?"

I can't deal with this. A month has passed since I left Mark, but nothing has changed. This girl is judging a situation she knows nothing about. I turn hard eyes on Julie as my nostrils flare.

"I didn't land either," I say through gritted teeth. "They both fucked me over, and I ended up so broken that I can barely function. But I guess some people might consider that lucky."

Lizzie looks at me with surprise in her eyes. "We need to talk," she says. She stands even though the plate in front of her is filled with food. She walks over to me and tugs my elbow. "Come with me."

She pulls me up and doesn't let go of my arm. We stalk through the buffet and out into the casino. We walk until we end up in some deserted hallway.

"You can barely function?" she finally asks, letting go of her grasp on me. Her eyes are wide and full of concern.

I lift a shoulder and swipe at yet another goddamn tear as it tracks down my cheek.

"Honey," she says gently, pulling me into a hug. "He's barely functioning, too. You two need to find your way back to each other."

"He pushed me toward Brian. Plus there was that girl at Sevens."

"What girl at Sevens?" Lizzie asks.

"That night he talked to you about me when we were all in Chicago. It was all over the internet. Jill texted me in the morning to ask if I'd seen it."

"What are you talking about?"

I grab my phone out of my clutch and pull up the article that broke my heart a month earlier. I hand her my phone with the first photo pulled up.

"What the hell?" she mutters. She cranes her neck and squints. She spreads her fingers over my screen to zoom in, and then she looks up at me. She smiles triumphantly and hands my phone back to me.

"Those aren't from that night."

"He admitted they were."

She raises both brows. "He said he met that chick after he talked to me?"

I shake my head, trying to remember his exact wording. "No. I asked him if it happened, and he said yes."

"Look at his hands."

"His hands?" My brows draw in, but I turn the phone back on and force myself to look at the pictures. I zoom in on the shot with the best view of his hands. "What about them?"

"He finished the sleeve on his left arm a couple months ago and decided to extend over the back of his hand. There's no tattoo on his hand in that photo."

"But what about the Sox hat? And the black shirt? It's the same shirt he was wearing when he left."

"You don't think that could all be added to the picture later? Do you really believe everything you see in pictures, Reese?"

My eyes meet hers. "I've never had a reason not to."

"Well, now you do."

"It doesn't even matter." It does, though. This proves Mark lied to me. It proves he actively worked to ruin things between us, and I'm left to assume the reason was because he was too scared to get into something real with me. "I just want to move forward. Besides, he and Brian can't fix their relationship if I'm in the picture."

She rolls her eyes. "After what Brian did, he doesn't deserve Mark's forgiveness as far as I'm concerned. Brian's the one who took a shit on everything, not Mark."

"Mark pursued me before he knew Brian's real motives. I'm sure that's all Brian's thinking about."

"It's in the past. You and Mark belong together."

"It doesn't matter who belongs where. The fact is it's over, and that's that. I'm just trying to move on, and to be honest, this is why I didn't want to come tonight." I start to walk away from her, away from this conversation and back to my dinner plate, but her soft voice is so full of fear that it stops me cold.

"Reese, I'm worried about him."

I turn back to face her, and I really look at her for the first time. I see tension beneath her eyes where I didn't notice it before. I see the way her brows are drawn together, causing her forehead to wrinkle. I watch as she twists a few strands of her hair between her fingers. What she's feeling goes deeper than just *worry*. She's fearful of what could happen, and I so badly want to ask what's going on—what he's doing that's causing her so much anxiety.

But I don't think I can take knowing the truth. I'm happier in this land of ignorance where we've each started the process of moving on with our own lives…or at least where we're pretending to.

I don't say anything, just stare blankly across the small space at her.

"I've never seen him like this, and I'm so afraid for him. I'm so afraid he's going to do something stupid."

Like what? You haven't seen him like what? You're afraid he's going to do...what?

These questions flash through my mind, but I don't ask them. As much as I wish things were different, they're not. I care about him, of course, and I want him to find happiness. But this isn't a clean break. This isn't the one thing I asked for when I abided by his wishes by jetting out of Chicago.

I draw in a deep breath, and I don't ask any of the questions in my head. Instead, I turn and head back toward the restaurant, leaving the bride to be staring after me with all that anguish for her brother in her eyes.

* * *

The nightclub isn't fun. All I can do is think about Lizzie's words. Music blares around us, bodies bump into me, girls laugh as their drinks splash over the sides of their glasses. I want to laugh at the girls dancing beside our group drinking daiquiris, the clear drink of choice of the younger crowd and the girls who are here on fake IDs, but I can't muster up any of the glee that causes a laugh. I want to have fun, but Lizzie's words war with my own good sense.

Jill is wine drunk, oblivious to my internal struggle. When I got back to the table after my talk with Lizzie in the hallway, Jill had a fresh glass of wine in her hand. It disappeared before I had the chance to pull her aside, to tell her I wanted to go home.

I'm dancing with the girls and going through the motions, but my heart isn't in it. My heart is stuck on a rooftop in Chicago.

I don't even bother to excuse myself when the need to just get out of here for a few minutes overwhelms me.

I beeline toward the doorway leading to the library room. It's connected to the main club, a quiet room. I don't know if I need special access to go in, but I slip past the security guard sitting outside it.

People mill around, and I remember the last time I was here. I sat in the chair in the corner with Brian as he slid his hand up my dress—slid it further up than he'd ever slid it before. We barely knew each other, but I wanted it to happen. I remember the thrills darting through me that this gorgeous and successful man wanted me. While he never drove Mark out of my head completely, he created a diversion, a way for me to see I could eventually get over the one night I shared with a rock star.

God, how naïve I was.

I walk over toward the bookcases and pull my phone out of my purse. I open my Uber app and put in my ride request. Then I head back to the loud room and hug Lizzie. "I need to get out of here," I say.

She stops dancing and stops smiling. "Don't go."

"I have to."

"Can I see you tomorrow?"

"I don't know if that's a good idea."

"Too bad." She gives me a drunken smile. "I'm coming over and you can't stop me."

God, the apple doesn't fall far from the tree in this family.

I say my goodbyes to Lizzie's friends and tell Jill I'm leaving. She follows me out.

"Don't go," she pleads.

"If you're having fun, you stay. I'm just bringing down everyone's good time."

"That's not true."

I roll my eyes. "That Julie girl won't stop looking at me with daggers in her eyes."

"Why?"

"We may have exchanged words when you went to the bathroom."

She giggles, a sound that tells me she's more than just a *little* wine drunk now.

"Call Beck. He'll love coming to pick up his drunk girlfriend."

She shakes her head. "We have our last night tonight."

Right. It's our last night in our house together. I'm moving out tomorrow, and she's moving out Sunday. We had big plans to have one final girl's night to celebrate all the years we've lived together.

But right now, I sort of just want to be alone.

"It's okay, Jill. Have some fun tonight. We'll have a sleepover another time."

"Who's coming to get you?"

"Uber."

She clears her throat. "Have you thought about calling him?"

"Who?"

"You know who."

"No, I haven't," I answer. It's a lie. I think a hundred times every day about calling him, about texting him, about getting in touch with him. Still, even after a month has passed—even after he kicked me out.

"Maybe you should."

"What am I supposed to do? Just call him up out of the blue and say, 'I know we said love isn't enough, but you wanna give it another go?'"

She lifts a shoulder. "I don't know the answer, Reese. But I know you." She pauses, and then she lets fly everything she's been protecting me from as she begins rambling. "I know you're miserable. I know you're not yourself. I know you're avoiding me and everyone who loves you. I just want you to be okay. I just want to be here for you."

"I'm fine." I know I'm being a bitch, but I don't want to talk about Mark anymore. I don't want to think about him anymore. I just want my life back.

She doesn't say anything for a few beats, and then she presses her lips together and nods her head. She blows out a breath. "Okay. You keep pushing away everyone who cares about you. You keep doing what you need to do to fix whatever they broke. No matter what, I'll still be here to help when you're finally ready to pick up the pieces."

She turns on her heel and heads back toward the club, and I'm left wondering what happened to my best friend...and why I suddenly feel like I'm the one in the wrong here.

ten

"You look like shit."

I think about slamming the door in Lizzie's face for that comment, but instead I just leave it open and walk over to collapse on my couch. I hear the door close and watch as she walks toward me in her cute leggings and tank top combo. She looks perky and fresh while I'm in pajama pants and an oversized t-shirt.

"Welcome to my home," I say once I'm situated with my head back on the pillows and burrowed under my blanket. Soon this won't be my home anymore—soon as in later today. The blanket and pillows are some of the last things left I need to pack. I slept on the couch last night because I already packed my sheets and took apart my bed frame.

I think of the card that fell out of a notebook when I was packing my desk yesterday. I brush it off, though Gram's words reverberate through my mind. *Another second apart from the man you belong with is one more second you don't get to share with each other, and that's a downright shame.*

She perches on the chair across from me. "What's with the boxes?" she asks.

"I'm moving."

She looks surprised. "When?"

"Tonight, actually."

"Oh," she says, her face falling. "So you won't make it to dinner tonight?"

I shake my head. I could probably swing it in terms of time, but it's too hard. I didn't have fun last night, and I know it'll be another night on the Strip with Mark's condo looming large just down the street.

"Where are you moving?"

"I'm staying with a friend until I figure out what I want to do. Indefinitely for now."

"Why?"

"Jill's moving in with Becker and our lease is up."

"You don't just want to stay here?" she asks.

"Of course I do. I love this house. But I can't afford the rent." It seems like something she can't understand. Whether or not she makes good money at her own job, she has a very generous brother with far more money than he can spend on his own. Surely money is something no one in the Fox family ever has to worry about.

"Get your ass up," she says as she stands.

"No thanks. I'm not buying whatever you're selling."

She rolls her eyes. "I didn't come all this way for you to ignore me."

"Then why did you come?"

"Well, for one thing, I still want you to come to the wedding."

"I can't." My response is immediate.

"Why not?"

"Crazy thing called airfare. I can't just fly out to Chicago. I can't afford a hotel."

"I'll take care of it."

"I'm not your charity case."

"Don't be a bitch." She narrows her eyes at me.

I love her for giving it to me straight as much as I hate her for the same reason.

"I care about you, Reese. You were there when Pops died. You held my hand as we prayed together. A bond born from tragedy lasts forever, so you're stuck with me."

"Great," I mutter, and she giggles.

"I know we don't know each other that well, but leaving both my brothers out of it for a minute, I care about you. I feel like you're the sister I always wanted and never had."

"That's a sweet thing to say, Liz, but I don't think it's a good idea." I clutch the blanket tightly against me, my only security as I think about who else will be at her wedding.

She changes the subject. "Have you been like this since you got home from Chicago?"

I sit up and shrug. "I've felt a little lonely."

"You have me." She gives me a big smile.

"You're leaving me to go back home tomorrow night."

"You have Jill."

I roll my eyes. "She's always at Becker's or working."

"You have your job."

"Which sucks. It's like whoever's in charge of kids' schedules said, 'Let's fuck with Reese this year and put all the bad kids in the same class.' I hate my job."

"Do you really hate your job?" she asks. "Or do you have a broken heart and you're not allowing yourself to enjoy anything because of the misery?"

I sigh heavily. "I don't know," I mutter.

"We've got to snap you out of this. What about a puppy? Puppies don't let you down."

"I don't want a puppy unless it's Max."

"You met Max?"

I nod.

"When?"

"Mark took me to LA. That's where we were when he got the call from your mom that Pops had a heart attack. Brian was calling me at the same time."

She furrows a brow. "I didn't know that."

"Which part?"

"Any of it. And with Max, well, Mark just..." She shakes her head. "He doesn't do that. He doesn't introduce women to Max. That's his baby."

"Who takes care of Max when Mark's away?"

"He has a dog sitter. He usually texts to let her know when he'll be in town and she drops Max at the house, or sometimes she'll stay at Mark's place to take care of the dog there."

"She?" I ask as I realize I'm jealous of a fucking dog sitter.

Lizzie giggles. "Yeah, *she*. Our seventeen-year-old cousin Abby."

"Fine. I'll let that one slide." We're both quiet for a beat, and then I finally ask the question that's been weighing on me since she mentioned it last night. "Why are you worried about him?"

"He was in Chicago last week. I hadn't seen him since the funeral, but he looked like shit. He lost weight. He looked like he hasn't slept in weeks. He was withdrawn and quiet, but not quiet like in a peaceful way, quiet in like a cagey way."

"Cagey?"

She lifts a shoulder. "I don't know how else to explain it. Something's going on with him."

"Was Brian there when you saw him?"

She shakes her head. "He was here in Vegas. He's kept himself busy with work."

"Have they spoken?" I know I'm asking a lot of questions, but I need the answers. I need to know if they've made up, if they're talking to each other, if the fact that Mark forced me to leave opened up any doors for two brothers to mend fences. I'm close with my sister, and I can't imagine my life without her in it. I don't want to. They may have an unhealthy competition, but I hate to see a family torn apart, and I hate even more that I'm at the root of the issue.

"Not since the funeral. At least not to my knowledge."

"What happened at the funeral?" I ask.

"It was afterward. We were at my parents' house and my dad forced them to talk to each other."

"Oh, God."

She nods. "It got pretty ugly."

"Has he been with other women?" I ask. I know better than to believe what I've seen on Twitter.

She lifts a shoulder. "I don't honestly know. But if you've seen the pictures, don't worry about them. Penny's just making sure he maintains his status as a womanizer. She had a lot of work to do after he was spotted with his arm around Gram, you know. Can't make him look too sensitive or too sweet." She shakes her finger at me like she's scolding a child.

"But he is," I say.

She tilts her head. "You know that and I know that, but the general public sees him as a tough bad boy who sleeps around for sport. If Penny didn't throw out some old pictures of him canoodling the ladies, people might get the wrong idea."

"Canoodling?"

She laughs. "You have a better word for it?"

"Fondling?"

"Gross." She makes a face. "That's my brother."

"Sexing?"

"Might be even worse than fondling." She waves a hand in the air. "The point is those are old images, at least as far as I know."

"What about the snap?"

She looks at me like I'm crazy.

"He sent a Snapchat a few weeks ago with him and another woman. They looked awfully cozy, and snaps are current images. You can't send one of an old picture."

"Mark doesn't know how to use Snapchat," she says, rolling her eyes and waving her hand dismissively.

I nod. "Yeah, he does. I taught him."

Her brows furrow. "You did? How long did that take?"

I giggle and sit up, feeling a little lighter as I reminisce about one of my favorite memories of my time with Mark. "Nearly a five-hour car ride from Phoenix to Vegas."

She laughs, too. "He's not the most adept at technology."

"He didn't understand the filters. I had to show him all the different ones and then I had to explain what happens when you post to My Story instead of just sending it to individuals." I ignore the twinge of regret I feel that we'll never recapture that moment.

"He probably messed up and meant to send whatever it was just to his friends."

"Regardless, I can't help but wonder who it was."

She squints at me as she thinks. "When did you say it was?"

"It was the day I got back home from visiting my parents in Phoenix. He didn't waste any time finding someone new."

"I doubt that, Reese. He was pretty broken up that day between you, Brian, Gramps, and Steve."

"Steve?"

She shakes her head. "Never mind. What did she look like?"

"Tell me," I demand.

She averts her eyes to the window. "There's some stuff going on with the band. It's personal and I can't talk about it."

"Is everything okay?"

She lifts a shoulder. "I don't know." Her voice is soft, but she's got me on high alert. "Tell me what the girl in the snap looked like."

I blow out a breath, pissed she won't tell me more and worried about Mark. "She had this long, straight, copper-colored hair and brown eyes. That's all I remember. Oh, they were cheek to cheek and they both looked a little drunk."

Lizzie thinks for a few beats. She pulls out her phone, taps some buttons, and scrolls around. Then she turns her screen around and passes her phone to me. "Is that her?"

One quick glance at the image makes me nauseous. It's Lizzie and the same girl. I nod.

She laughs. "That's Penny. Mark's publicist."

"Penny? As in the woman who releases all the pictures of Mark canoodling women?"

She nods. "Yeah. And I promise, there's nothing sexual between them."

"You don't know that."

"Uh, yeah, I do."

I narrow my eyes at her. "How?"

"She's related."

"Oh."

She laughs. "She's my dad's cousin's daughter. Does that make her a second cousin?" She furrows her brow then shakes her head like it doesn't matter when she just blew my whole world apart. "I don't know," she says, waving her hand in the air again. "We grew up with her, and when the band first started, she did free publicity for them as part of her intern project for school. They started getting popular about the same time she finished her degree. She moved to LA, gained some other clients, and the rest is history."

"Thanks for clearing that up."

"I wish I could tell you more, but he didn't open up to me when I saw him. All I know is he looked like shit. He's not doing well. And," she nods to the blanket I'm burrowed under, "neither are you. He needs you as much as you need him."

"Everyone keeps saying that, but I don't have any options."

"There are always options, Reese."

"But he's the one who asked me to leave. Am I supposed to beg him to take me back when he told me love isn't enough? I have to protect myself."

"Protect yourself all you want." She stands up and sticks her clutch under her arm. She motions to me with her other hand. "Look where it's getting you." She walks toward my front door. "I need to go pay a visit to my idiot brother Butt-head. I'll see you in October." She wiggles her fingers in a little wave and disappears out my door before I have the chance to protest.

eleven

Justin shows up at my door a few hours later with a U-Haul truck, two of his friends, and a girl I've never seen before.

"You remember Tim and Karl," he says, nodding to his friends. "And this is Alex." She's short and petite with black, chin-length hair and big, brown eyes. She's adorable and she and Justin make an attractive couple.

"Nice to meet you," I say, sticking my hand out to shake Alex's. "Thank you for coming to help."

I can't help but wonder if she came to help so she could check out the ex, but she quells those thoughts.

"Justin has told me so much about you," she says with a warm smile that makes me like her. She's a stronger woman than I am. I wouldn't like the idea of my boyfriend hanging out with his ex.

I observe the dynamic between Justin and Alex as we all work to get my belongings on the moving truck. He's different with her—different than he was with me. It's the way he looks at her. He never looked at me like that, and while we did have something special and we shared a lot of love, it's clear she's the love of his life.

Jill's home to help with some of my stuff, and I'll be back tomorrow to help her with hers. I wish we would've had our little celebration of our last night in our place together, but I have enough regrets I'm trying to battle. I don't need to add that to the list.

She's quiet, passing by me without talking to me as we both carry boxes to the truck. I think she's mad at me. Either that, or she's silently judging the fact that Justin is the one here helping me. I don't want to argue with her, so I don't say anything.

I hate this is how Jill and I are leaving things between us after living together for almost a decade, but if she's going to be mad at me for something stupid, then I can be mad at her for being the reason I have to move in the first place.

We get everything packed in the truck—including my couch blankets and pillows—and I drive my car by myself while Justin takes his crew in the truck to Tess's place. Jill doesn't join us. Instead, she tells us how she needs to stay back to pack a few of her own boxes.

Once everything is unloaded, I treat Justin, Alex, Tim, and Karl to beer and pizza. Tess showers and heads out for a Saturday night with some of her friends. She invites me, but I just want to stay in and get myself settled.

When I have the essentials unpacked and my bed made, I finally lie down and scroll my phone. I see a new Snapchat posted on Mark's story, another pose with a different woman sent just an hour ago. Bile rises in my throat, but, being the masochist I am, I log onto Twitter out of curiosity just to see what city he's in. I'm attacked by a steady stream of images, all the same but all with different women. Some are with Ethan, and in one from just last night, he's kissing a blonde woman. His hand is on her neck, and black ink snakes along his skin. My heart's already shattered, but another piece somehow chips off.

I remind myself it's Penny posting these, Lizzie's words that they're old images.

The reminder doesn't help...it still hurts. Maybe he has moved on. Maybe these are real.

I head back to the old house to help Jill the next morning. She's alone in her bedroom with a few last-minute boxes.

"Where's Becker?" I ask.

"He had some work to do this morning. He's coming back with a truck in a few hours."

"Can we talk?"

She nods but doesn't stop packing. I sit on the edge of her stripped mattress.

"I'm sorry I took my shit out on you," I say.

She glances up at me and then her gaze returns to her task. "It's okay, Reese. You know I love you no matter what. Can I ask you something?"

I raise my brows.

"Why was Justin helping you?"

"He offered."

"Is it smart to hang out with an ex?"

I sigh. "He's different. He's got a new girlfriend, and after everything that went down, I just don't have those feelings for him anymore."

"I'm proud of you," she says softly.

"For what?"

"For moving forward. Focusing ahead. I know it's not easy."

I give her a tight smile. "It's not, but it's my only option."

When Jill's all moved out of our place and I give her my key to drop at the realtor's office this week, I head back to Tess's place. I'm not surprised to see Jason sitting on the couch watching a baseball game, but I *am* surprised to see Brian Fox sitting beside him.

My heart wrenches in my chest. Is this what it's going to be like to live here? Because if it is, I don't think I'll be able to stay here long.

Brian glances up at me when I walk in. His face is healed, completely restored back to its original attractiveness, but we all wear scars on our insides now for different reasons. "Hey," he says casually, as if he didn't use me for sex for months in some convoluted effort to get revenge on his brother.

"What are you doing here?" I ask.

"Watching the Sox win." He says it as a joke, like I care about baseball. I don't. I'm much more of a football gal, but the Sox immediately make me think of Mark and that hat and the woman behind Sevens he lied about.

I walk into the kitchen and pour myself a glass of wine. I will *not* be made to feel intimidated in my own home. Moving in with Tess was a bad idea. My two closest friends are dating Brian's two closest friends, and that proximity makes me uncomfortable.

"Where's Tess?" I ask.

"Shower," Jason says, his eyes not moving from the television screen.

I sit on a chair across the room from Brian. I feel his eyes on me, but I refuse to look at him. He finally stands and moves across the room, taking a seat on the end of the couch closest to me. "How've you been, Reese?" he asks.

I take a sip of wine and press my lips together. "Fine." The single word is short and I keep my eyes on the television.

"You doing okay with the move?" he asks.

"Yeah."

"Doing okay with everything else?"

I finally tear my eyes from the screen to focus on him. "If you mean the fact that you used me for months, no, I'm not okay with that. If you mean whether I'm okay with you coming between Mark and me, nope, still not okay. So, no. I'm not doing okay with everything else, and I fully blame you for that."

"I'm sorry," he says softly. I see Jason's eyes edge from the television in our direction.

"What are you really doing here?" I ask. "Is this a thing? Do you hang out here a lot?"

He lifts a shoulder. "Not a lot. Jason mentioned you were moving in with Tess and I wanted to check on you."

"Thanks for your concern, but it's not your business."

"It used to be," he says softly.

I nod. "Yeah, it did. Before I knew how much you were screwing me over." With those as my parting words and the image of regret in Brian's eyes, I get up and go to my bedroom.

twelve

Homecoming weekend is a huge deal at my school, and as I pin curls into place on my head for tonight's ball, I think back to when I met Brian to beg him to donate to our fundraiser for this very weekend. I brush the thought away. I don't want Brian in my head, especially not after seeing him sitting on Tess's couch last weekend.

I don't have a date for tonight's ball, but I have Tess, who decided to bring Jason, and I know Justin will be there with Alex. Since the Homecoming football game is Friday night and the kids' dance is Saturday, the black-tie ball and auction for adults is Thursday. This year, the grand prize is a Toyota Tacoma, but there's trips and concert tickets and all sorts of goodies up for grabs.

I feel like Cinderella in my gown as I walk into the banquet hall located just minutes from my school. I make my way to the bar first—it's an after school function and there aren't any kids around.

I bump into Justin and Alex, who promise to sit at my table, and then I find Tess and Jason. As I talk to the two of them, my heart races as I spot dark hair and green eyes across the room chatting with my principal.

And it doesn't race in a good way.

"What the hell is he doing here?" I ask.

Jason and Tess follow my line of sight, and as if he can feel our eyes on him, Brian turns and spots us.

"Since he was the single largest donor, they offered him a free meal," Jason explains.

I blow out a frustrated breath. "He didn't have to take it."

"I'm pretty sure there was more than one reason he did." Jason's voice is quiet.

"Spill it," I say.

He looks uncomfortable. "He wants to talk to you."

I roll my eyes. "How nice of him to attack me first at my home and then at a work function."

"It's not an attack, Reese," Jason says.

Tess puts her arm around my shoulders. "We're here for you, babe."

I don't even get a chance to respond because Brian starts making his way over to us.

"Hey," he says softly.

"We'll leave you alone," Jason says, tugging Tess's arm. I give her a pleading look, but she follows Jason to the bar. So much for her parting words of *we're here for you.*

"What are you doing here?" I blurt before he has a chance to speak. I avoid looking directly at him as I pretend to survey the room.

"I owe you an apology."

"You owe me more than that." My words taste bitter on my tongue.

"You're right."

I take a sip of wine for strength. "I'd like my dignity back, for one."

"What I did is unforgivable, and I fully admit that. I was acting from a place of jealousy and hatred, and you got caught in the crossfire. For that, I apologize."

"It's not okay." I look around the room and absentmindedly recognize some people.

"I don't deserve your forgiveness."

"You're damn right about that."

Brian sighs. "I hate this—I hate that my brother won't talk to me, I hate that you hate me. I hate that I screwed you over so badly. You never deserved that, Reese."

I cut him off again. "Blah blah blah. Like I believe a damn word out of your lying mouth."

He looks wounded as he blows out a sigh. "I donated the Tacoma."

My eyes dart to his. We both know the car will bring in a ton of auction money, and it was generous of him.

But I can't help the cynical part of me that believes it all stems back to Mark. Brian didn't donate anything except someone else's money.

"I wish your brother was here." The words are out before I can stop them. I know I'm saying them to hurt him, but there's so much truth behind them that even I can hear the pining in my own voice. I'd love it if he were here—love to see what he had to say to someone who damaged everything we held so close to our hearts. I'd love to see him and rush into his arms and beg him to take me back.

Brian's eyes flash with hurt, and I feel a little dart of satisfaction that I put it there.

"I'm worried about him, Reese." His voice is low as he says the words just as I turn to leave, but I still catch the apprehension in it. It matches Lizzie's tone when she expressed the same concerns to me, but it's not my problem anymore and I can't let it be for someone who wrote me out of his life.

I hurry across the room toward the table where I find Justin and Alex.

"What's wrong?" Justin asks when I slide into the empty seat next to him.

"My ex is here."

Alex laughs. "You're sitting next to him."

I can't help my small smile. "A more recent ex."

"Mark? Or Brian?" Justin asks.

"You've dated two guys since Justin?" Alex asks. She looks impressed.

"Brothers," Justin whispers to her.

I roll my eyes. "It's a long story."

Alex looks around. "This sounds interesting."

I give her the short version. "I met a guy, liked him, but we didn't exchange numbers. Then I met a new guy, started dating him, and found out he's the first guy's brother. In the end, the second brother orchestrated our entire relationship as a way to get revenge on his brother."

"So which one is here?" Alex asks.

I fiddle with the stem of my wineglass. "The one who used me to get revenge."

"Want me to kick his ass?" Justin asks.

I glance over at Brian and then back at Justin. I narrow my eyes.

"What?" Justin says. "You don't think I could take him?"

I make a face and Alex laughs just as Jason and Tess join us. To my complete and utter horror, Brian pulls out the chair next to Jason. Before he sits, he reaches across the table to shake Justin's hand.

"Brian Fox," he says politely.

"Justin Nolan. And this is my girlfriend, Alex Russell."

"Nice to meet you," Brian says as he sits.

Well this is certainly a scenario I never imagined. I remember thinking it would be strange to sit at a Thanksgiving dinner next to one brother while I pined for the other. I remember thinking Mark and I would share passionate glances across the table while Brian sat beside me.

In all those wild scenarios, I never imagined sitting at a school function next to Justin while Brian sat across the table from us as I pined for Mark.

A few awkward beats pass, and then Tess eases the tension by asking how Justin's classes are going. He launches into a long spiel about how hard his kids have been working, and we lose Brian and Jason to their own work conversation.

When the interminable dinner finally ends, it's time for the auction. This is the biggest fundraiser of the entire year, and the top ticket item is Brian's donation.

Or so I thought.

The truck goes for a cool thirty thousand, but then Mr. Monroe says he has one final item up for auction.

"I've managed to keep this item a secret, but it's the biggest valued item we've ever had. It doesn't have a retail price on it, but I've been told it goes for upwards of four hundred thousand dollars."

My ears perk up as I wonder who donated such a valuable item.

"When I was first approached about this item, I didn't even know the person who called me. I had to ask my daughter, but she filled me in. Apparently, he's the lead singer of a very popular band."

My heart thumps and I close my eyes.

I know. I immediately know who the singer is, and I can suddenly hear my pulse beating in my ears.

"Let me hear a cheer if you've heard of the band Vail!" Mr. Monroe says.

The crowded room erupts in noise. Once the cheers die down a little, he says, "Our final auction item tonight is a private performance from the lead singer of Vail, Mark Ashton!"

Screams of excitement carry all around the room. I see people turning to those next to them as they figure out a way to pool their money together to win this once in a lifetime experience.

No one could possibly know what's going through my head. Or my stomach, for that matter, which suddenly feels like it wants to toss its contents.

Did he do this for me? Did he do it when we were together or was it after I left him in Chicago? Is he trying to tell me something? And if he is...what is it?

I don't know, but I need to get out of here.

"I'd like to start the bidding at twenty-five thousand dollars," Mr. Monroe says as I stand. I see someone in the back of the room raise a hand as I move toward the door.

More hands go up as I pass by, but it's all a blur. I don't know who is bidding or how high the bids go or who will win a private performance with the man I love. I want that performance—just like everyone else in the room does, but I can't afford it.

I can't afford it monetarily, obviously, but worse, I can't afford it emotionally. I step outside for some fresh air when I feel a hand on my arm.

I turn around and find myself face to face with Alex. Frankly, I'm a little surprised she's the one who came out to see if I'm okay—not my roommate, Tess. Not my ex, Brian. Not even my ex-who's-now-a-friend, Justin, for that matter. But Alex.

"Are you okay?" she asks.

I draw in a deep breath and nod. "Yeah. I'm okay."

"It has to be weird sitting at the same table as two of your exes."

I nod and shoot her a wry smile. "It's a little weird, but I don't have those feelings for either of them anymore." I don't go beyond that, don't get into the real reason why I couldn't sit at that table for a second longer.

"Because of the brother?" she guesses.

"Yeah," I say vaguely, still not admitting who he is or how much the last auction item affected me. "I'm kind of hung up on him."

"That's what Justin told me."

"I think I'm going to head home. I put in my time. Will you be at the game tomorrow?"

She nods.

"I'll see you there. Say bye to Justin for me, okay?"

"I will." She leans in for a quick hug, and it's odd how much she feels like a friend even though she's the new woman in my ex-boyfriend's life. It's nice to have a stable friendship since it feels like everyone else is abandoning me in different ways.

thirteen

The song on the radio that breaks into my thoughts as I drive home from work on a Friday afternoon sounds a lot like Vail, but I've never heard it before. By the time I realize it's Mark singing, the song is over. When the deejay announces that it's a solo single from Mark Ashton titled "Only Ever You," I pull into the nearest parking lot, find it on my music app, and buy it immediately.

This time I really listen as Mark's words wash over me.

You want me to let go, want me to leave
Told me you loved him, wanted him, needed him
But I couldn't do it
Because it was only ever you

You told me to write about somebody else
then broke down in my arms, in my house, in my heart
I held you close to me
Because it was only ever you

You left me alone after a trying goodbye
Thought you'd run back to me, please come back to me
I need you now more than ever
Because it will only ever be you

Tears are streaming down my face in the middle of a parking lot as I listen to the words he wrote about me, about us. About our end and about how he still needs me.

I wonder when he wrote the song, when he recorded it and released it. Why he released it solo instead of with Vail. Did he write it before or after he kicked me out of Chicago? Is he doing a solo album? I think back to Lizzie's words about Steve. Something is going on with the band, but it's something I'm not privy to.

And that's how it should be. I don't deserve to know because I'm not part of his life anymore.

None of this is the solace I was seeking when I unwillingly left Chicago. He keeps coming back to haunt me, keeps coming back like a bad penny or the hair on my legs or the pile of laundry I need to do, and I think it's because the two of us belong together. I'm just not sure how to get him back when he's the one who ended it.

I blow out a breath as the tears start to subside. I clutch those last words to my heart. *It will only ever be you.*

A text comes through on my phone.

Justin: *Alex wants to take you somewhere tonight. You free?*

Me: *Where?*

Justin: *Can't tell you, but you'll like it. Promise.*

Me: *Please tell me it's not a double date.*

Justin: *Okay, it's not a double date.*

Me: *Please tell me it's not a threesome.*

Justin: *Damn, you guessed it.*

Me: *Not interested.*

Justin: *No offense, but I don't think Alex would be into that. Invite Jill, too. We'll pick you up at seven.*

I'm curious what they've planned, but I don't ask any more questions. I focus on trying to feel a little excitement for plans with friends instead of all the other chaos going on in my life at the moment.

I call Jill as I resume driving. Her voice fills my car speakers.

"Hey stranger," she answers.

"Are you free tonight?"

"Beck's taking me to dinner. Why?"

"Justin just texted me that he and Alex want to take me somewhere tonight and they said to invite you. Please don't make me be a third wheel on their date."

"Justin and Alex?"

"Yeah."

"Are you, like, friends now?"

"Sort of. We hung out at the Homecoming ball and then the game the next night. She's sweet."

"And what about Justin?"

"What about him?"

She blows out a breath. "Are you still in love with him?"

I laugh. "No. I mean, part of me will always love him, sure. But my heart is firmly planted in Mark's hands, and I sort of just need to be on my own for a while."

"Promise?"

"Promise."

"Okay. I'll cancel with Beck and meet you at your place. What time?"

"They're coming at seven. Come early so we can pre-game."

She laughs. "I'll bring the booze."

"Deal."

We hang up, and I can't help but think how much I miss my best friend.

I pull into Tess's apartment complex. This still doesn't feel like home.

I thought Tess and I might carpool and I'd find myself growing closer to her. Instead, I feel like a burden taking over her guest room. I'll take what I can get for now, but I need to find a permanent solution.

She's not home when I walk in, which isn't all that unusual. She's been spending a lot of time with Jason, though she denies they're getting serious.

I have no idea what's planned for tonight, but I want to be comfortable. I pull on a pair of jeans, pair them with a black shirt, and slide my feet into my Converse.

I hear a knock at the door a few minutes later. "Your captain is here," Jill says when I open the door, holding up a bottle of Captain Morgan.

We each have a few sips, and then another knock lets us know Justin and Alex are here. We share our rum, and then it's off to our night of fun, wherever that may lead us.

We drive toward the Strip but take a left instead of a right off the highway. Justin pulls his car into the parking deck of The Palms, and the four of us get out of the car.

The second we step onto the elevator, my heart thumps in my chest.

There's a poster in the elevator advertising tonight's entertainment at their music venue.

One Night Only: VAIL.

I'm momentarily mesmerized by Mark's eyes as they stare back at me. I finally pull my eyes from Mark's to look at Justin as I feel Jill's hand on my shoulder. His eyes are twinkling, and I feel like I might vomit right here in this tiny elevator car.

"You didn't...we're not..." I stutter.

He nods as he grins, and then he pulls four tickets out of his back pocket. "Front row!" He's giddy with excitement. "Alex's dad is a big spender at the casino, and they comped him four tickets to tonight's show!"

"I can't." I back away from him and bump into the wall. I want to back further away but I can't. Goddamn small elevator.

Mark is somewhere in the building, sharing the same air as me, the same space. He's getting ready for his show.

I think of the toast with Jägermeister Morgan poured for everyone, and my mind drifts to Morgan for a second. I wonder if she knows what happened, if she misses the friendship we never got to have. I wonder if Angelique is smug in her knowledge that she was right—I was just another flash in the pan for Mark Ashton. I wonder if they're toasting now, if Mark is leading them. I wonder if some other woman is standing behind Mark, ready to kiss him before he goes onstage, ready to go home and warm the place beside him in his bed. I wonder if she'll tweet about him tonight or in the morning.

The thoughts are downright suffocating. I don't even notice the other three people with me because my eyes are back on Mark's in that advertisement. I'm about to tell Justin and Alex I need to get the fuck out of here when the elevator doors pop open.

"Are you okay?" Justin asks.

I don't answer as I follow him through the casino. Somewhere in my periphery, I hear Jill say something to him, but it doesn't register because a light up sign in the middle of the casino catches my eye. I'm drawn to the image displayed in the advertisement.

Mark stands in the center of the image with Ethan, Steve, and James flanked behind him. This one's different from the advertisement in the elevator. They're outside on some street with a blue sky extending forever behind them. Mark's green eyes blaze, and whoever edited this image needs a promotion. The ink on his arms is dark, a stark contrast to the brightness of the sky behind them. He's ferocious in this photo, like the man who took me to bed that night after the private performance in Los Angeles. I wish I knew when it was taken. I look at his hands—as I always do now because of Lizzie. The tattoos are there, which means this image was snapped within the past few months. I wonder if it was before me or after me or during me.

It doesn't change anything, but I'd love to know what caused those emotions I see so clearly behind his eyes. Was he thinking of me, of us? I can't name any of what's there other than pure *sex*, but it's a look he used in the privacy of a bedroom he shared with me. I wonder if it's the same look he gives *every* woman in the bedroom or if I truly was different for him.

After the way he made love to me my last day in Chicago, I have to believe I was different.

Jill grabs my arm to pull me out of my trance with this photograph of a man who is so much more to me than just the elusive rock star performing on a stage tonight.

I draw in a deep breath and look up at the ceiling to ward off the tears I know are starting to form. If I'm already emotional and we're not even inside the actual theater yet, I have no idea what's going to happen once I see him on that stage, once his voice attacks my auditory system.

I'm trying to figure out how to explain this to Justin and Alex as we step in front of the Pearl theater. A sign in front of the entry says, "Video Recording in Progress. By entering venue, you agree that your image and likeness may be recorded for commercial use."

"Is this okay?" Justin asks.

I clear my throat and look around wildly for a moment before I focus on his face. "The Mark I told you about, the one I dated and broke up with just a month ago—it's Mark Ashton."

His face goes white and his eyes widen. "Oh, shit."

I nod. "You couldn't have known."

"We don't have to go," Alex says.

I don't want to see Mark.

But I want to see Mark so bad it hurts.

The song I heard today on my way home plays in my head. *Only Ever You.* Does he still feel that way? Or was it just a song?

I don't have time to allow the emotions to war inside me, because Justin, Alex, and Jill are all waiting for me to respond. I'm sure they all want to go in to see the multi-platinum band perform, but I'm also sure none of them have any idea the things going on in my head right now.

"It's okay," I say, forcing a fake smile.

Justin hands our tickets to the attendant and we're waved inside. Another attendant leads us to our seats. "Usually Vail has a general admission on the floor," I say once we're seated. The row is full and we're the last to arrive.

Alex nods. "This is a special performance they're filming for some special on one of the music channels. I guess they've been on tour but this isn't technically one of the stops."

The theater goes dark on those words. Cheers rise up from the crowd in the darkness. The pluck of a guitar string causes the cheers to rise in a crescendo that becomes deafening squeals and screams all around me. Everyone in my row stands and moves against the wall separating us from the stage—including my friends and me.

A single light illuminates a lone figure in the center of the stage, and I immediately recognize his lean frame. Fog rises up from beneath him, casting him in a cloud lit only by a soft, blue light.

I stare at him, memorize him from where I stand. I'm not that far from him, yet somehow, I'm further than I've ever been at the same time. His eyes are focused on his instrument. He strums his fingers along the strings, and I recognize the song as one of my favorites. He gives it a good, long intro, and just before the first verse begins, bright lights flood the stage and the rest of the instruments join in—Ethan beats the drums, James slaps the bass, and Steve pounds another guitar all at the same time as Mark's voice starts the lyrics.

I draw in a breath as if I'm breathing him in. I can almost smell the sandalwood and peppermint from here if I try hard enough. I can almost feel his arms around me again.

Seeing him there in all his glory, professional as always, doing what he loves to do, doing what he lives for...it sends a shooting pain through my spine at the same time it starts to heal my heart. He's here. He's okay. He's doing well.

Maybe he's doing well without me, but that's beside the point. I've been living in this darkness, not allowing myself to move on—especially after Lizzie and Brian both told me they're worried about him—but I can see for myself just in the first five seconds of a fully lit stage that he's doing okay. He's surviving. He's singing the words I know so well, but I can't bring myself to sing along around the lump in my throat. People are dancing beside me and behind me. Justin sways to the beat on my right and Jill belts out the words on my left. The crowd pumps fists in the air in unison on the refrain as they shout the words, but I stand stock still as I watch him.

First impressions told me he was fine, but the longer I watch him, the more I start to find the cracks. I wonder if Morgan and Angelique are here, backstage critiquing or even doing it from here in the crowd somewhere. I glance around for them, but then I brush the thought aside as I listen to his voice. It's a tad grittier than normal. Maybe he has a cold, or it could be the sound system. My eyes trail down his body. He looks like he's lost some weight. I can't see his eyes, not from this distance, but I want to. I want to know if he looks tired and withdrawn up close like Lizzie said. Surely he's been beautified by some make-up artist for this television performance and I wouldn't be able to see those things in his eyes from down in the crowd.

The second and third songs are from their first album, but then they play a cover. I recognize the opening notes of "These Eyes" by the Guess Who. I listen as Mark puts his own twist on a classic song, as he sings the words about how he'll never find another love like he had.

With me? Is he talking about me, thinking about me as he sings those words? Or is his band just covering a golden oldie?

It's a sensual, smoky version of the song, slowed way down. His eyes are closed as his hand strokes the mic stand, up and down, up and down. He grips the microphone before he repeats the process. His voice gets deep and gritty, but then he bellows out the words with all the pent-up emotion of a man who lost the love of his life.

This is the Mark I know, the one who loves hard and passionately.

He's lost himself to the words, to the emotions, to the music. My heart aches.

"Are you okay?" Justin asks me.

I don't answer. I can't. I'm too mesmerized by what I'm seeing on the stage.

Justin mistakes my silence for not hearing him. He puts his arm around my shoulder to pull me a little closer to him so I can hear him when he asks again.

I nod without taking my eyes off the man in front of me, and that's when Mark's eyes finally find me. When he glances up from his focus on his guitar and his eyes meet mine for the first time since I left his condo in Chicago, actual tears begin to fall down my cheeks.

I watch as his eyes widen in surprise to see me here. I listen as some of the grit disappears from his voice and he pours still more emotion into the words, as if he's drawing strength from the line of vision connecting our eyes.

Is it just my imagination? Is it just that charming way he has about him, the way he commands a stage, the way he makes every person in the room feel like he's singing directly to them?

Hope blooms in my chest. I want to see him, want him to know I'm here watching him perform, want to know what he's thinking. I want to hold him, to kiss him, to tell him I'll always be his. Forever. We didn't screw this up. We can stop wasting time now. I was stupid to leave and he was stupid to push me away, but we can be smarter going forward.

Old emotions fire up in my chest—feelings I long buried with the death of what we had. Feelings I left on a rooftop in Chicago. Feelings that belong between Mark and me.

But then his eyes slide to the man beside me—the man whose arm is slung around me, and Mark's eyes darken. He focuses on everything and everyone around me after that, purposely avoiding my eyes.

He introduces a new song, one I've never heard before.

"This is from our upcoming album. It's called 'Until You.'"

He strums his guitar, a single light on the stage only on him, just like when the concert began. He bellows out the first few bars, and then his eyes meet mine again. I hang onto every single syllable as his voice fills with pent-up emotions he never shares with anyone yet somehow shares with everyone through his music.

I didn't know what love was, didn't know what pain was
Until you
I didn't know what love was, didn't know what hate was
Until you

He glances away from me after he repeats the refrain. His words claw at me as I know without a doubt he's talking about me.

I gave you a part of me, showed you what no one else could see
I let you in and held you tight, loved you all throughout the night
I handed you my trust, and it left me feeling crushed

I didn't know what love was, didn't know what pain was
Until you
I didn't know what love was, didn't know what hate was
Until you

I didn't deserve you anyway, told you that one fated day
Now I know why I never do this, and even though I still feel your kiss
I can't think of you anymore, it's the one thing I know for sure

I don't know if there are more lyrics because my instinct is to flee. I can't listen to more of his words, not when I know who they're about. Not when I know he wrote them thinking of me—hating me or loving me or something in between.

I wind up in the bathroom, Jill close on my tail as sobs erupt out of my chest. *I can't think of you anymore.*

He can't even bear to *think* of me anymore. What does that say about the hope I allowed myself to feel for a few glorious moments? I'm a fucking idiot, that's what it says.

Jill rubs my back, but it does nothing to comfort me. I just want to be alone. I push her away from me. "I need to get out of here," I manage to say between the sobs that rack my body.

"Stay," she says. "It'll be okay."

"Stay? Are you kidding me? Did you fucking hear what he just said?" My voice is hysterical and loud and women are looking at us with curiosity but I couldn't give a fuck.

"I heard," Jill says softly, soothingly. "It just means he isn't over you."

"He said he hates me. He said he didn't know what hate was until me." Those loud words draw a few more curious glances.

She puts her hands on my biceps to try to steady me, but it doesn't work.

"Maybe he didn't mean you," she says. "Maybe he meant his brother."

"Bullshit. He meant me. I can't be here, Jill. He wrote an entire song about how I fucked him up. Stay if you want, but I'm done here."

I head out of the bathroom. I hear cheering as I make my way up some stairs and find myself out in the casino. Justin and Alex are waiting near the theater's entrance.

"I'm so sorry," Alex says. She pulls me into a hug. "I had no idea."

I shake my head. "You couldn't have known. I never told either of you."

Justin ducks his head sheepishly. "Are you okay?" he asks.

I shrug.

"I'm so sorry. I thought seeing your favorite band would be fun," he says.

I press my lips together. "It would've been back before I met him."

"Do you want to talk about it?" Alex asks.

I shake my head. "I'd just like to go home."

fourteen

Justin pulls into Tess's apartment complex and drops Jill and me off.

"I know we haven't had much time to chat lately, and I'm sorry for that," Jill says as we stand outside the door and I fumble for my keys. I'm reminded of the time I fumbled through my purse for my sunglasses then quite literally bumped into Brian Fox. "I'll make time. I love you and I miss you."

I hug my best friend. "I love you, too. Thank you for coming tonight." I slide the key into the door, and when I open it, I find my roommate on the couch.

With a guy.

Nearly naked.

Having what sounds like pretty good sex.

Oh, and it's not Jason.

They don't seem disturbed at all by the fact that the door has opened. I look at Jill and roll my eyes, and she just shakes her head. I close the door and back away. I have no idea how long Tess's fuck fest is going to last, but I don't want to sit inside while I wait for it to end. We walk over to the stairs leading up to the second floor apartments and sit next to each other on the third step.

"Come stay with Beck and me."

I shake my head. "You don't want me there. It might actually keep you from banging on your couch whenever you want."

She laughs. "You need to move."

"I know. I hardly ever see her, but when I do, she's either having sex or just finished having it. You don't really know someone until you live with them, you know?"

"Poor Jason."

I rest my elbows on my knees and rub my forehead with both palms. "How long do you think we need to wait out here?"

"She sounded like she was getting close."

"She always sounds like that." I just want to crawl into bed after the fucked up night I've had.

Jill chuckles. "How'd it feel to see him?" she asks softly after a few quiet beats.

I glance over at her then turn my gaze down to the ground. "It felt..." I shake my head. "It felt good to see him, to know he's okay. I had a minute there where I felt all this hope for us, but then..." I trail off as I remember the words and the emotion he poured into them. I lift a shoulder. "He wrote an entire song about how much I fucked him up."

She slings her arm around my shoulders in a side hug. "I'm sorry, Reese. I'm sorry I haven't been here for you through this."

I shake my head. "I shouldn't have pushed you away, but you were moving and it was easier to deal with it by being mad."

"You're welcome at our place," she says.

"I appreciate that. I'll figure something out."

We're quiet for a minute, and then she stands. "Come with me."

"It's okay, Jill."

"We're not going to my house. I have somewhere special I'm taking you."

I follow wordlessly to her car since my other option is walking past my roommate having sex on the couch. She drives for a few minutes and then we end up at the International House of Pancakes.

"IHOP!" I exclaim once we get there.

Pancakes were our thing back in high school. We'd go almost every Friday night, sit in a booth with pancakes and coffee, and chat. Sometimes it was just the two of us, and other times we had a big group of friends. We haven't done this in ages, and the memories of a simpler time bring an immediate smile to my face.

She grins at me and gets out of the car. I scramble to follow her inside, glad to have my best friend back.

* * *

When Monday rolls around, I'm hoping for work to be a distraction.

It's not.

Thoughts of Mark on that stage haunt me as my seniors work on a timed essay during the last period of the day. I don't even care about what happened with Justin—it's Mark that I can't seem to get out of my head.

My phone starts vibrating in my pocket when there's just a few minutes left in class. Who would be calling me during school hours? I leave my phone in my pocket, hating the impatience I feel at not knowing who it is. The buzzing stops, and there's no follow-up buzz, so whoever called didn't leave a message.

When the bell rings and the last student leaves the room, I finally slip my phone out of my pocket to see who the missed call is from.

Brian Fox.

Why the hell would Brian Fox be calling me?

There's no voicemail, no text message. There's just one random missed phone call from Brian Fox sitting on my screen. He might think I ignored the call, might think I purposely didn't answer when I saw it was him. Good—I hope he does think that. If I would've seen his name flash across my screen and been able to get to it in time to answer, I wouldn't have picked up his call anyway.

A tremor of fear darts through my belly. What if something's wrong?

That tremor follows me as I go through my end of the day routine. I pick up bits of paper kids dropped on the floor, gather a stray pencil and stick it in the box in the front of my room. I erase my white board in the silence of an empty classroom. I finalize my slides for tomorrow's lecture.

The whole time, that tremor sits in the pit of my stomach as it spreads like an infection to my bloodstream. By the time I've finished paperclipping today's essays together and dreading the scoring process, my entire body is tense with anxiety and I'm almost convinced I should call him back.

Why the hell did Brian Fox call me? Why didn't he leave a message?

I begin drafting a text message.

Saw your call.

I backspace and start over.

Did you mean to call me?

That doesn't work either.

Is something wrong?

Maybe he's just looking for Jason and since I live with Tess, he tried me. That doesn't even make sense, and besides, if he was just looking for Jason, he'd have texted. If he needed the shirt he left behind that I threw away when I moved out of the house I shared with Jill, he'd have texted. If he had some other trivial question, he'd have texted.

He didn't text. This isn't something trivial.

Something's wrong. It's the only explanation. It's the only reason he'd pick up a phone and purposely dial my number after what he did to me.

It's Mark. I feel it in my bones. Something's wrong with Mark. Something bad happened.

I always used to think bad things only happened in the middle of the night.

My mom used to worry about me when I was in college and told her we'd left our apartment at ten or eleven the night before to go out. She'd always tell me, "Bad things happen in the middle of the night."

I ignored her at the time, but she wasn't wrong.

I think back to those simple college days, when the biggest decision of my day was whether I wanted to drink rum or vodka that night.

When Shelby Anderson drank too much and had to have her stomach pumped, guess what time it was? It certainly wasn't noon. When Johnny Bates was arrested for getting into a fight at a bar, guess what time it was? It wasn't dinnertime.

But right now, it's not the middle of the night. I hold onto the false sense of security in the daylight as I look out the window for a beat at the cloudless sky and the palm trees just outside.

I avert my eyes from the window and open a browser on my phone. I search *Mark Ashton* and click the *news* button.

I read the headline from the first article—it's from this morning: *Bad Boy Mark Ashton Hospitalized with Exhaustion.*

My chest tightens with a sob so thick I can't even get it out. I choke on something in the back of my throat.

Exhaustion.

I know what that means. It wasn't exhaustion last time, and I'm terrified it isn't this time, either.

I push my pride aside. Brian Fox called me after everything that happened between the three of us, and I can't think of a single *good* reason he'd do that—especially considering that article. I scroll desperately through the headlines to find some update that says he's released or doing better, but everything I find is vague and says the same goddamn thing.

Exhaustion.

Bile rises in the back of my throat as I sit at my desk and stare at Brian's contact in my phone. I dialed this number so easily so many times in the past, but now I can't bring myself to click the button. I can't bring myself back into their fold. I want Mark to be okay with everything in my being. Not knowing is torture, but I'm terrified that knowing could be even worse.

I glance at the clock on the top of my phone. Forty-six minutes have passed since he called.

My phone starts buzzing in my palm, and I nearly drop it as it startles me. My heart races as it takes me a second to put together the fact that I'm receiving an incoming call. I stare at the name on my screen.

Brian Fox.

I accept the call with a deep breath.

"Hello?"

"Reese, hi. It's, uh, Brian Fox."

"I know."

"I wasn't sure if you deleted my number."

I don't respond. I can't talk around the lump in my throat, and my heart's still racing. It won't slow down, and I'm scared as we make small talk.

He sighs heavily. "I'm calling because of Mark."

"Is he okay?" I whisper.

"No." His voice breaks on the single word, and I'm not sure I'm equipped to handle this conversation. My breath falls out of me like I've been punched in the stomach.

I can't deal with this.

He's not okay? I just saw him on Friday. He didn't look great, but he looked *okay* at least.

What happened since then? I'm so stunned at that single word that I can't even cry, not yet.

"But I think he will be," Brian says. His voice is full of emotion that shocks me into needing to keep him on the line.

I swallow, try to clear my throat, but nothing helps to dislodge the lump back there. I finally manage to ask, "What happened?"

Brian clears his throat, too, as he tries to talk around his emotions. "He mixed some things last night that caused him to black out. They're calling it an overdose."

"What did he mix?"

"Weed, scotch, and morphine."

"God." I blow out a breath. "Why are you telling me this?"

He doesn't answer my question. "He's in Chicago and I think you need to go see him."

"Why?" I whisper.

"He's on a path of destruction, and it's because of me and what I did to you." His voice breaks again. "I know I fucked up, okay? I know I took it too far. I think you might be the only one who can get through to him."

"He won't want me there."

His voice is low and comforting when he speaks. "Of course he will. He combined enough drugs to black out, but he could've taken enough to kill himself. He didn't. He's still breathing, and where there's breath, there's hope."

Tears fill my eyes as he recites the very words that were in my own mind not all that long ago. "How do I get in to see him?"

"You'll need to go in with someone on his approved visitor list."

"Are you on it?" I ask.

He clears his throat. "No." His voice is distant. I can't tell if he's angry about that or not, but I don't believe he has any right to feel anger over it.

"Who is?"

"Ethan, Steve, James, Vick, Vinny, and Penny."

"Not Liz?"

"No family. I'm sure he doesn't want us to know the truth."

"But you know?"

"Yeah."

I don't ask how because it doesn't seem important. The only thing that *does* seem important is getting to Mark as quickly as I can. I need to see him with my own two eyes. I need to watch the rise and fall of his chest and know he's still here—even if it doesn't mean we ever have the chance to be together. "I don't know how to get in touch with any of them."

"It's a good thing I do, then."

* * *

I speed home to pack a bag with enough of my belongings to get me through two nights and then I speed to the airport and book a seat on the first flight to Chicago.

I busy myself on the flight with lesson plans for the next two days. I don't know if I'll need more time beyond that—hell, I don't even know if I'll need to stay in Chicago for two whole days. All I know is I need to get to him.

There's a car waiting for me at the airport. Brian told me he'd arrange it for me, and—surprisingly—he didn't let me down. I stare out the window at the scenery as the car takes me from the airport to the hospital. I focus on emailing my lesson plans from my phone and putting in for a substitute for the next two days so it'll be off my plate.

When we finally arrive at the same hospital where Pops passed away not so long ago, I text Vinny. Brian gave me his number, and he's the one who'll get me in to see Mark.

Vinny meets me at the entrance with a nod. "Ms. Brady."

It's the second time Vinny has ever spoken to me, but for some reason, it fills me with a well of relief. I throw my arms around him. "It's so good to see you, Vinny."

He huffs out a breath, not really a chuckle, but not really *not* one, either, then turns to walk into the building. He leads me toward Mark's room.

I just saw him a few nights ago when he performed on a stage in front of me, but I didn't really *see* him.

I'm scared. I don't know what I'm walking into, don't know what to expect.

"How's he doing?" I ask.

"Exhausted," Vinny says pointedly.

I nod, desperate for more—desperate for the truth. But I understand his meaning: we shouldn't talk out here.

We wind through a series of hallways until we find his floor. Each step matches the pounding echo of my heart.

We walk all the way down to the very last door where a uniformed police officer sits. He eyes me shrewdly and nods to Vinny, who reaches for the doorknob.

"You ready?" Vinny asks me.

I lift a shoulder. How can you ever prepare for this moment? How can you ever be ready to see the person you love more than anyone or anything in the world sitting in a bed in a hospital because he's self-destructing?

He nods then opens the door.

My eyes instantly meet Mark's across the room. He's connected to an IV and his head rests against a pillow, but he sits up a little straighter when he sees me. He looks like my

Mark, though he looks like an exhausted, weaker version of the man I love. The man I can't get out of my head because my heart won't allow it. His eyes are sunken deep into his pale face. The normal vibrancy and charisma are replaced with the haunting look of a man who's completely lost.

He looks away from me as he refocuses his eyes out the window. "What are you doing here?" His tone is blunt but his voice is weak. The rasp I recognized behind his lyrics on Friday night was because of whatever this is. This doesn't look anything like the strong man I fell for after one night.

Seeing him like this—like the man I love but at the same time *not*—causes the fissures in my heart that I thought might be starting to mend to split wide open again.

"Exhaustion?" I ask, going for a light tone. I expect him to give me some sort of acknowledgment, a wry smile or even a look of shame to validate my innuendo, but all he does is lift a shoulder without looking at me.

I glance around the huge hospital room. Only the best for a celebrity who needs help, I suppose.

A nurse is busy with a stack of papers near a counter on one side of the room. She's young and blonde and pretty and I hate that he's in here with her. She glances over at me but keeps doing whatever she's doing. Vinny steps back out into the hallway to give us the illusion of privacy.

I force one foot in front of the other. This is hard, but whatever demons he's battling are worse than what's going on in my head. Whatever put him here is harder, and suddenly I'm desperate to be the one he unloads that on. I thought once upon a time that I couldn't be strong enough to shoulder his issues, that we'd need to face them together, but maybe I'm stronger than I've given myself credit for.

I look at his bed—I want to sit there, but I'm not sure how welcome it would be. I choose the chair next to the bed instead. I reach for his hand, but he pulls it away.

"You shouldn't be here," he says.

"I agree."

He finally blows out a breath and his green eyes fall to mine, those same green eyes I love, but they're different today. "Who told you?"

"You ready for this one?" I press my lips together.

He lifts both brows.

"Brian."

He shakes his head. "How does he even know?"

"I didn't ask. He's worried about you."

He ignores my words. "You were there on Friday." He says it like a fact, not a question.

I nod slowly. "The tickets were a surprise from a friend who thought I'd love to see my favorite band from the front row."

"But you ran out. Our new shit's not *that* bad is it?" A glimmer of my sweet Mark shines through this new version at his teasing tone.

"I loved seeing you there," I say softly as I pick at a fingernail that doesn't need picking. "But 'Until You' was kind of rough."

"Rough like it needed work?"

I shake my head. "Rough like it was hard to hear."

His brows draw down. "A love song that was hard to hear?"

"That was a love song? You said you didn't know what hate was until you met me."

"Didn't you listen to the last verse?"

"I left somewhere around 'I can't think of you anymore.'"

His eyes soften for just a beat, but then his gaze returns to the window. "You should've stayed." He doesn't expand on that, and I can't help but wonder about the rest of the song.

"What are you doing to yourself, Mark?"

"Trying to find something that makes me feel as good as the last hit I took."

"If you're trying to make a joke, it's a bad one."

He levels his gaze at me, and there's not a trace of joking behind his sad eyes. "I was talking about you."

"Oh." Like some bumbling fool, it's all I can think of to say.

We're both quiet, and I look out the same window he's returned his gaze to. After everything we went through, it's hard to believe we can't come up with anything to say to each other right now.

"People are worried about you. Your sister—"

"Thinks she knows everything. She doesn't," he says, interrupting me. His voice is cold and hard. The nurse glances over at us.

"That's not what I was going to say."

He holds out a hand as if to tell me to continue.

"She's been worried about you for a while. She told me to get in touch with you."

"Why didn't you?" he asks. His voice is flat, and I can't tell if he's asking because he wanted me to or if he's asking because he's genuinely curious why I didn't.

"You basically kicked me out of Chicago and told me you needed to focus on your family. What was I supposed to do?"

He doesn't answer as he rests his head back on his pillow. "I need to sleep. I'm in here for exhaustion."

"Understandable. I've heard drinking and marijuana can make you tired, but mixing morphine on top of that must make you downright exhausted."

He presses his lips together, not responding to my words yet at the same time acknowledging the truth of what I said—that I know the real reason he's in here.

"Two depressants mixed with liquor would exhaust anyone," I say.

"I don't need another goddamn lecture." His voice is sharp—sharper than I'd expect in his weakened state, and the nurse glances over at us again. He looks at her. "Can you give us a minute?" he asks her.

"I'll just be a few more minutes, Mr. Ashton," she says. "And I need to check your bags before I go."

He blows out a frustrated breath and nods over toward the nurse. "Becky's just making sure I'm not going to hurt myself. Or you."

"You already hurt me once," I say softly. "Give me your worst."

His eyes soften again, and I feel like I might be getting through to him.

"Can I ask you a question?" I ask.

"That was a question."

I roll my eyes. "I'm serious."

He nods.

"You have it all, Mark. You have everything going for you—talent, money, fame. Why are you on this path of self-destruction?"

He shakes his head and looks at me pointedly. "Because I don't have everything." He lowers his voice and breaks our eye contact.

I catch his hidden meaning, and it breaks my heart.

I stand from my chair and sit on the edge of his bed. I take one of his hands between both of mine. It's ice cold—a temperature I'd never associate with Mark. "I'm right here, and I'm not going anywhere."

He blows out a breath and closes his eyes. Becky steps over and does something to his IV bag before tapping some information into a computer.

His breathing evens out, and by the time Becky leaves the room, he's asleep.

I hold his hand as I sit on his bed, staring at the man I love as I wonder where the hell we go from here.

fifteen

"What the fuck are you doing here?" Ethan's sharp voice pulls me out of my thoughts.

Mark has been sleeping for the last hour as I've sat on his bed and held his hand. I carefully untangle my fingers from his and stand. I walk across the room toward Ethan as I sort of feel like I've stepped into a movie. It's so weird to be in the same room as two people whose performances I've admired for over a decade. One's half in love with me, I think, and the other hates my very existence.

"Brian told me he was here," I say quietly.

"You're the reason he's here." Ethan's eyes are hard and his voice is cold.

I close my eyes in pain for a beat at his words. I know he's just lashing out, but he's not wrong. This is my fault. Mark admitted as much when he said he was looking for something that makes him feel the same way I made him feel. "I know. And I'm going to make it right."

"How?"

"Look, you're not exactly innocent."

He narrows his eyes at me.

"He told me about the last time he was hospitalized for exhaustion."

I don't miss the surprise that flashes through his eyes, but our conversation is cut short when Becky walks back into the room. "Is he still sleeping?" she asks. She glances at her watch.

I nod.

"This is the first time he's slept for more than a few minutes since he got here," she says. She looks at Ethan and points at him with a glare. "Don't you dare wake him up, Ethan Fuller."

He grins at her with innocence, and it's easy to see how he and Mark together make one hell of a team. Both devastatingly handsome bad boys with a proclivity for sex.

Becky rolls her eyes and looks at me. "He seemed to instantly calm when you walked in. Keep doing whatever you're doing." She heads over to the counter to flip through her paperwork again.

I give Ethan a pointed glare then walk back to the bed. I sit in the chair beside it and slide my phone out of my pocket. Ethan collapses on a couch by the windows, but I don't pay attention to him.

Mark jolts awake in the bed a few minutes later. I drop my phone with a clatter onto the table beside his bed and stand as he pants out a breath.

"Are you okay?" I ask. Becky rushes over.

He looks gratefully at me and nods. "Some water, please." His voice is dry and scratchy from sleep, and I hand him the cup sitting beside my phone. He gulps it down and hands the cup back to me, and Becky starts poking and prodding at him to check his vitals.

"When the fuck can I go home?" he growls at her.

"We're keeping you one more night for observation, but if everything looks good in the morning, you'll be released then."

He groans in annoyance. "I was hoping to get out tonight."

Becky shoots him an apologetic smile. "Sorry Charlie."

"His name's Mark," Ethan says.

Becky rolls her eyes. "I know. Haven't you ever heard that phrase? *Sorry Charlie*?"

Ethan just stares at her blankly. "I've heard of the phrase *bedside manner from a hot nurse*."

"Smooth, Fuller," Mark says.

Becky blushes and taps some notes on the computer.

"How do I keep my mother out of here another night?" Mark asks. I'm not sure if he's talking to me, Ethan, Becky, or himself.

"Why do you want to keep your mom out?" I ask.

He glances up at me. "I don't want her to know the real reason I'm in here."

"No one will say a word if you want her here," Becky says without glancing up from the screen.

He blows out a heavy sigh. "*Want* is such a strong word."

I giggle, but his mom *should* be here for her son.

"I'll text Liz," he says.

I'm nervous as I watch him contact his family to let them know they can come visit. I'm terrified to see Diane again, excited to see Lizzie, wondering if Gram and Paul will come, too. Maybe I should leave. I don't know what this means, that I'm here with Mark and about to see his family again—does it even mean anything?

All I know is the second Brian told me where Mark was, I needed to be by his side. Whether or not that has significance remains to be seen, and right now that's not the focus. Getting Mark out of this hospital needs to be our sole focus. Everything else can come later.

Ethan takes off and Lizzie arrives shortly after. Her eyes speak of the surprise she feels in seeing me here, but she gives me a big hug. "Exhaustion?" she asks Mark, rolling her eyes.

He nods with innocence, and I get the feeling she knows the truth just like Brian did. Mark likes to act like the big, strong brother who doesn't want his younger siblings to know the truth, but they know. He has weaknesses just like everyone despite his status as a god of rock.

"You look like shit," she says, and I giggle.

"I hate you," he tells her, but the affection in his voice betrays his real feelings.

"Hope you're getting plenty of sleep in here because you look like you need it."

"Get out," he says, and she ignores him as she plops down on the bed.

"When are they springing you from this joint?" she asks.

"Tomorrow." He glances at the nurse. "I figured I couldn't keep mom out another night."

"She's been blowing up my phone about why you couldn't have visitors. Fair warning, you may want to fake sleep when she gets here." Lizzie turns back to me. "You have somewhere to stay tonight?"

"I, uh, haven't thought that far ahead to be honest." I figured I'd just crash in Mark's hospital room.

"Stay with me." She says it like a command, not like an invitation, so I'm sort of trapped into it. It'll be nice, though, to stay with someone who feels like a friend.

I glance over at Mark, and he just shrugs at me like he can't stop the steamroll of his sister any more than I can.

"I don't want to be a burden," I say as a weak protest.

"Then I'll put you to work." Lizzie grins at me.

The door is thrown open and Diane's voice fills the room. "Oh, Mark!" She flies through over to her son and—just as Lizzie predicted—smothers him. "You look terrible!"

Paul walks in next and his surprised eyes fall on me. I smile awkwardly at him.

"How have you been, Reese?" he asks softly.

I lift a shoulder as I wonder exactly how much he knows about what happened between me and his two sons. "Hanging in there."

"What are you doing here?"

My eyes fall on Mark as his mother fawns over him. I decide to give Brian the credit he deserves here. "Brian called to tell me Mark needed me, and I dropped everything."

"Thank you," he says, giving my forearm a squeeze. "I'm not sure either of my sons deserves you."

I glance at the floor as heat creeps into my cheeks. "That's nice of you to say."

"How's he doing?" Paul asks. We both glance over at him. Diane's talking quietly the way a mother does to soothe her thirty-four-year-old child, and he looks both miserable and exhausted.

I tiptoe around what happened but I'm blunt with the truth. "He needs rest. It's been busy since I got here and I'm sure it won't slow down."

"We won't stay long. When Diane got the text from Mark that he was cleared for visitors, we were on our way home from an evening out."

I nod, and he goes over to join his wife and son. Lizzie steps closer to me so we can have a quiet conversation of our own.

"How *are* you?" she asks softly.

"I'm not sure," I say. "It's not every day your ex-boyfriend calls you to let you know his brother, who also happens to be your other ex, is in the hospital halfway across the country."

"But you're here. What does that mean?"

I glance over at Mark, and our eyes lock across the room. "I don't know what it means. I don't know if it means anything at all."

* * *

Lizzie has to leave to get ready for work tomorrow, and she takes me home with her. I don't hug Mark, don't kiss him when I say goodbye, and it feels like something's missing. It's just a simple goodbye when I want it to be so much more. I have so much I want to say to him, but I have no idea where to begin. Since Lizzie is dragging me with her back to her place, I don't get the chance to talk to him alone.

I chuckle at the photo of Mark and Brian standing next to Beavis and Butt-head that greets me near her entry. Dave is watching ESPN just like the last time I walked into this condo.

"How is he?" he asks. He turns off the television.

Lizzie shrugs, and I'm still wondering how much they know. "He looked like shit but he's getting sprung in the morning."

"You do know what getting sprung means, don't you?" Dave asks her.

"It's like getting released from the hospital." She flips her hair back haughtily.

Dave grins. "It also means getting a boner."

She rolls her eyes and looks pointedly at me. "We have company."

"Don't let me stop you," I say.

Dave winks at me. "I knew I always liked you."

Lizzie takes me back to the guest room I stayed in the night Brian confessed and Mark kicked his ass. She brings me towels and asks if I need anything else as I set my bag on the dresser.

"I'm fine, but I know I'll be restless. Is there anything I can do?"

She nods. "I've got a little over a month until the wedding. There's *always* stuff to do."

I giggle and she sits on the bed.

"Before we get to all that, though, talk to me."

"About what?"

"What's going on? Why's he really in the hospital?"

I play dumb and shrug.

"Same reason as last time?" she asks.

"Exhaustion," I say.

She nods. "Okay. We both know that's bullshit, but if you're not going to tell me..."

"Brian said he mixed some things and overdosed."

She shakes her head and averts her eyes to the floor. "I knew he was on this stupid path and I didn't know how to stop him." She looks up at me. "I hope you can get through to him."

I sit beside her. "I hope I can, too. But just because I'm here...I don't know if it changes anything."

"I'm scared for him, Reese. I don't want to lose him to something so stupid." Her voice is passionate, and I take her hand in mine and give it a squeeze.

"We won't."

She nods. "You think you might get back together?"

I shrug. "I have no idea. But I'm here, and that's the first step."

"I'm happy you're here."

"I am, too. Now how can I help with wedding stuff?"

She leads me to the kitchen, where there's a mass of mesh fabric cut into perfect circles, about ten pounds of those gross hard almond candies in a soft teal color, and pre-cut ribbons with *David & Elizabeth* printed on one side and the wedding date printed on the other.

She counts out ten almonds, places them in one of the meshy circles, and shows me how to tie the bows so none of the text is covered up. "You sure you don't mind doing this?" she asks.

I shake my head, and she leaves me alone with my thoughts as she and her fiancé head to bed.

sixteen

Mark's Chicago driver Todd takes me to the hospital in the morning. I head that way when Lizzie and Dave leave to get to work. I don't want to hang around their condo all day by myself, and I'm anxious to get back to Mark after a night of very little sleep.

When I walk back into his hospital room, I have the urge to run to him. He's sitting on the edge of the bed. The IVs have been removed and he's starting to look more like himself. I hang back by the door because I don't know the rules here.

"Come here," he says softly. I walk over toward him, and when I get close enough, he grabs me by my hips and pulls me close. He rests his cheek against my stomach, and it's such an intimate and emotional moment that I want to live inside it forever.

By no means do I think this equates a reconciliation, but I do have hope in my heart it could lead us back to a place I thought I'd never see again.

We're interrupted by the morning shift nurse, who hands Mark a bunch of paperwork and fills him in on what to do at home. Ethan shows up a few minutes later, and before I know it, Todd is speeding through the streets of Chicago as we head from the hospital back to Mark's place in the back of a black Yukon. Vinny got Mark a Bears hat, and he's wearing it down low—so low that even if his eyes weren't covered by sunglasses, I wouldn't be able to see them.

Ethan sat beside him when we got into the back of the car, so we're not posed in my preferred position as we make our way toward Mark's place. It's less than twenty minutes, but it feels like a lifetime. Ethan talks to Mark about some gigs they've had to postpone. I wring my hands silently when I really want to scream at Ethan to shut the fuck up. Mark needs a break from work without worrying about everything he's missed.

I know it's not exhaustion that landed him in the hospital, but he still *looks* like he's exhausted and he needs rest. Chatting about work might be the only way Ethan knows how to deal with this, but he's acting like everything's normal when Mark is dealing with the recovery of a fucking *drug overdose.* I'm not sure Ethan fully realizes or appreciates the implications that come with that, but then again, Ethan's the one who thinks he's invincible.

I feel like a very unnecessary third wheel as we pull up to Mark's building. A line of people stands off to one side behind some caution tape, and Mark blows out a breath. Vinny opens the back door and Mark tugs on the bill of his ballcap, but it's already down as far as it can go.

"You ready?" Vinny asks.

I can't see Mark's eyes, but I feel him look at me. "Keep your head down and stay close," he says softly.

Ethan gets out first and holds up his arms in front of the line of people, who I quickly discover are photographers.

Paparazzi. In front of Mark Ashton's home.

People who want the first picture of the man who was just released from the hospital due to *exhaustion.*

Mark gets out next, and Vinny stands in front of him to do his best to shield him from the cameras.

I get out last and follow closely behind Mark, just as he told me to. He links his arm around my waist, and I grab on tight to him to help steady him. I'm a little scared with this first real paparazzi experience, but I hold onto him mostly because I'm desperate to feel him against me.

I keep my head down even though I want to look at them. I want to put faces to the people who are invading Mark's privacy. I want to know who they are, why they think taking a picture of a sick man somehow deserves the massive payday they'll surely get. I want to know where the hell their ethics are. These are the same types of people who stood at a man's funeral to get pictures of Mark with his grandmother.

My chest feels heavy as I think of all the implications here. He doesn't have the luxury of privacy. His life is splashed across the tabloids—and it's not even really his life. It's what Penny says his life is.

We're able to get past the crowd of people and into the lobby fairly quickly. I reluctantly drop my arm from around him once we're inside, and the four of us step onto an elevator car alone. A woman tries to get on, but Vinny denies her entry.

Mark leans on the mirrored wall of the elevator and rests his head back with a small thud. I wish I could see his eyes, wish I had some indication of what he's thinking.

I expect that once we're inside, Vinny and Ethan will leave and we'll have some time alone. He can rest, or we can talk. We'll do whatever he's ready to do.

Except that choice is stripped from us when we open the door and find Steve and James sitting at the kitchen table while Morgan and Angelique chat over on the couch.

Morgan squeals when we walk in. She darts across the room and pulls me into a hug. "I'm so happy to see you again."

"You, too," I say.

I meet Angelique's stare from across the room, but she glances away quickly. She clearly doesn't share the same sentiment as Morgan.

My eyes find Mark. He's pinching the bridge of his nose like he's on the verge of a breakdown.

"Can I get you anything?" I ask him softly.

His gaze falls on me, and I swear I see a hint of heat fire up his eyes. "I can get it."

"Please, let me." I set my palm on his forearm. "What do you need?"

"A beer."

I laugh. "No."

He rolls his eyes. "Fine, then. Some water."

I bring Mark some water, and he's discussing some reworking of their schedule with Vick and some guy I've never seen before on video chat when there's a knock at the door.

Alone. I just want five minutes alone with Mark, yet here come more people.

I glance over at the door wondering if I should get that or if someone else will. I'm not exactly sure of my place here. Am I here as Mark's girlfriend? Not really—we haven't discussed it.

Because I can't get a goddamn minute alone with him.

"I'll get it," Morgan says.

My attention is pulled from my thoughts when I hear shrieking. I glance up to see a trim, gorgeous woman with copper hair flinging her arms around Mark. *Who the fuck is she?*

The copper hair is familiar, and when she turns around, I recognize her from the Snapchat Mark sent that turned my world upside down.

"Thank God you're finally here, Pen." Mark's voice has gained some strength as he's surrounded by some of the most important people in his life, and I have no right to feel jealous as he hugs the copper-headed beauty close to his chest. "Where the fuck have you been?" He pushes out of their embrace and holds her around her biceps. He gives her a silly little shake.

"Cleaning up your mess, you fucking idiot." She smacks him in the arm. "What the hell were you thinking?"

He rubs his arm in jest, but then his eyes meet mine from across the room. He blows out a breath. "I wasn't thinking."

Her eyes follow his over to me. She slips her arm around his waist as he tosses his arm around her shoulder. She leans into him and acts like what she's saying is just for him, but I still hear it even over the music and across the room. "I assume that's Reese?"

She knows who I am?

I finally push aside my insecurities and gather up the strength to walk over to them. "Reese Brady," I say, sticking out my hand to shake hers. Up close, she's gorgeous with a smattering of freckles over her nose and her wide, innocent eyes that are a glittering blue.

"It's so nice to finally meet you," she says, leaving Mark's side to step over to me. "I'm Penny."

So this is the infamous *Penny*. I'm torn on whether to love or hate this woman. She's saved Mark's image on multiple occasions, but she's also painted him the way she wants—or at least the way that'll sell the most records. But that's also her just doing her job, and clearly, she does it well.

"Nice to meet you," I say, glad to know pretty Penny and Mark are related, even if they're distant relatives. I don't want the image of them having sex in my head, and the fact that they're related helps obliterate it.

She gives me a genuine smile then turns back to Mark. "When can you get back to work?"

"I feel fine now," he says.

I decide to interject. "The nurse said to give it a few days."

Penny's head whips over to me and Ethan glares at me. Penny turns slowly from me to Mark. "Friday, then?"

"I'd probably give it through the weekend," I say. "But he can go to his doctor sooner to see if he has medical clearance."

I feel awkward as all eyes land on me, but I was in the room when the nurse gave him his release instructions.

"*Through the weekend?*" Penny says as her eyes widen.

I look at the people around the room—people who love him, of course, but people who also depend on him for more than just a steady paycheck.

Mark sighs. "I'm fine."

I shake my head. It may not be my place to interject, but I care about his health. That's more important to me than a few awkward glances in my direction if I'm overstepping my bounds. "You've been out of the hospital all of an hour. You're not *fine*."

"We have studio time booked Wednesday in Nashville," Steve says. "Will you make that?"

Everyone looks at *me* to answer—everyone except Mark. "Yeah, I'll be there. We're just laying tracks. I'll be sitting all day."

Penny sighs. "You'll be traveling to get there and then working, and that's not stress you need right now."

He rolls his eyes petulantly and Penny looks over at me with a bit of sympathy. I think I might love her.

"All right, Vail," she says. "Get your asses out of here. Mark and I have work to do and you're distracting him."

I open my mouth to protest, to tell her he *can't* work right now, but Penny shoots me a look that clearly tells me to shut up.

Everyone groans, but they do what they're told. The boys all say their goodbyes to Mark. Steve and James both give me hugs, as does Morgan, and they all file out.

Mark ambles over to the couch and collapses on it, stretching his legs out across the cushions. "Where do we start?" he asks Penny. I stand in the kitchen like an outsider, so

I sit at the table and scroll my phone while I pretend like I'm not listening to every word.

"You have to get better," she says, walking over toward him. She perches on the coffee table in front of the couch. "And that's it for now. I've got the rest."

"But you said we have work to do."

"I said that to get everyone out of here. We do, we always do, obviously, but it can wait. I'll bear the load for now."

"We've already cancelled two shows because of this mess, and if I can't leave my house, we'll have to cancel more." His voice is desperate.

"People will understand that your health comes first. Let me worry about the schedule. You worry about getting healthy."

Mark blows out a frustrated breath.

"I'll release a statement in the morning about how I saw you and you're doing much better," Penny says. "I'll push off Nashville but won't cancel anything beyond Thursday. We'll see how you're feeling. Maybe I can sort through the paps' pics from when you got here earlier and pay someone for an exclusive. Most of them are already all over the gossip sites, though."

"Pen, people are gonna forget about us." I can't see his face—he's looking out the windows and I'm behind him in the kitchen, but I hear the fear in his voice even from here.

"No, Mark. They'll *never* forget you. Don't you get that? There's a group of teenaged girls in Minneapolis who organized a candlelight vigil to pray for you. It went viral. I have thousands of unopened cards at the office for you. Tweets and retweets, campaigns on every social media network to send positive vibes. You were trending on Facebook last night. Honey, people will not forget you. They just want you better, and going to the studio to lay tracks on Wednesday is a stupid idea. You need your voice at a thousand percent to lay tracks on an album. You know that. You're still suffering from lethargy. I can hear it in your voice. It's strained. Give it a few days, drink a bucket of tea every day, shoot down honey and lemon if you need to."

Penny glances over at me, and I silently mouth *thank you* to her when our eyes meet. She presses her lips together in a small smile and nods.

"Honey and lemon in large quantities will give me the shits."

I can't help the laugh that bubbles out of me at that. So much for pretending not to listen.

"Then don't do that," Penny says. "Unless you think it'll help."

Mark runs his hand through his hair. "This was really fucking stupid."

"I can't argue with you there. You ready to tell me what happened?" she asks.

He shakes his head. "Not really."

"Fine. When you're ready."

He lowers his voice, and I strain to hear. "Ethan wanted to smoke, so we smoked. I was having a rough time and weed makes the pain go away, right? It didn't, so I drank some scotch. Still didn't numb anything. I got my hands on some morphine and took that, too. Figured since it's a painkiller, it would kill the pain. I started to feel numb, but then I started having these crazy dreams and didn't know if I was awake or asleep. They say I started panicking, but I don't remember."

"Who gave you the morphine?"

"It doesn't matter."

She sighs, and we both know it was Ethan from that answer. "How'd you get to the hospital?"

"I don't know. I think James finally convinced Ethan I needed to go."

"Are you fucking dumb?" Penny asks.

I have to admit, I agree completely with her. She has the balls to say it to his face, though, and I like that about her.

He doesn't answer.

"Do you realize what you could've done? Look at Hendrix. Morrison. Winehouse. Weiland. Do you need me to go on?"

"Morrison died from heart failure." His voice is defeated with an argument so weak it's not even an argument.

"Suspected from heroin."

"I don't do heroin. I'm not stupid."

I realize I'm sitting stock still in the kitchen as I listen to their conversation. I shake my head and continue the pretense of scrolling through emails on my phone.

"Oh, but mixing with morphine is smart?" Penny asks. "You know that's what took Paul Gray from Slipknot and that guy from Def Leppard, right?"

He doesn't answer again, and now I'm positive I love her. She's one of the few people in the world who talks to Mark like this. His mother, his sister, and...me? We're the only ones, I think.

"What had you hurting so much?" she asks softly.

Mark doesn't answer with words, but I see his head nod in my direction. I'm trying to decipher if the head nod means he's blaming me or if it means he doesn't want to talk about it with me in the room.

Penny looks over at me, and my eyes fill with tears. Either way, it's my fault. I know deep down it isn't—it was an accident on the part of a grown man who was hurting, a bad decision that led to a terrible mistake. It could've been much worse, though—it could've cost him his life, but now we have the time to sort through it, time to get to the root of all that pain and find a way to begin to heal it.

"I need some time to talk to Reese," Mark says. "How long are you in town?"

"I have a return flight booked for Wednesday, but if you need me longer, I'll change it."

"You have other clients. I'll be fine."

She gives him a warning look, and he cowers a bit under her gaze. I giggle softly to myself as she stands to leave.

My heart races. This is it—*finally*. We're finally going to get some time alone after way too many days apart.

"Text me if you need anything," she says.

"I will." He reaches for his phone. "Fuck," he mutters. He glances up at me and blows out a frustrated breath.

"What?" Penny asks just as there's a knock at the door.

She walks over to get it while I busy myself with wiping down the counters. I realize Mark probably has a Chicago housekeeper much like Hazel in Vegas, but I need to feel like I'm doing *something*.

I can't help but glance over at the door—who the hell could it be now? Who would have a key card with access to Mark's floor that hasn't already been here?

Of course.

I hear Diane's voice as she pushes past Penny and rushes through the room over to her son. "You're looking better," she says.

Mark nods to me. "Because she's here."

My face heats at his words, but I pretend I don't hear them as I continue to wipe down the kitchen. Paul walks through the door a minute later with a bag of food. He ambles over to the kitchen table and spreads out a variety of soups, salads, and breads. "Anybody hungry?" he asks while Diane once again fawns over her son.

"He looks a lot better today. Doesn't he look a lot better, Paul?"

"He looks great," Paul says. He looks at me and rolls his eyes, and I stifle a snicker. I head over to the cabinet to pull out plates and silverware, and soon we're sitting around the table. Mark eats like he hasn't eaten in days, which, come to think of it, he probably hasn't. He eats two bowls of soup and almost an entire loaf of bread before he pats his stomach and tells us he couldn't eat another bite. Then he goes to work on a salad.

"Reese, don't you have to go to work?" Diane finally asks me.

"I took off a few days to be here with Mark," I say. I shred a piece of bread. "I'll stay as long as he needs me to."

"That isn't necessary. We're here to care for him now if you need to get back to Vegas."

"Knock it off," Mark says sharply.

Diane looks miffed to be scolded by her son, and I do my best to hide my smug smile, though I'm fairly sure I'm unsuccessful in that endeavor.

"I'm just saying we're here, so it's not necessary for her to be here if she has other things she needs to do." Diane purses her lips.

Mark sighs in frustration, and I can tell she's getting under his skin. "Why are you being rude, Mom?"

I glance over at Diane, who is the picture of innocence as a hand flies to her chest. "What? Me?"

Mark raises his brows pointedly, and Diane releases a breath.

"Fine. I just don't think she deserves you. Not after the stunts she pulled." She gives me a glare, and I want to ask what stunts at the same time I want to run the hell out of this penthouse as fast and far as I can.

"What stunts are those?" Mark asks the question in my head.

"Let's not do this now," I say, a hint of desperation in my voice.

"The whole thing with Brian," she says.

Paul watches us all like a damn tennis match, like he's not sure where to side. Siding against his wife will surely get him in trouble, but siding with her is a lie based on the things he said to me.

"Okay, we're doing this now, then," I mutter.

Mark rises from the table. "The whole thing with Brian was Brian's fault." His voice is a scary hiss and it's one part sexy and one part startling. "If you believe it's any other way than that, you're blind." He slams his fists on the table, and I jump.

"Mark, calm down," Paul says. "Your brother isn't even here to defend himself."

"There's no defense for what he did," Mark says icily. He walks over toward the windows and looks out over the busy city.

"What, exactly, did he do?" Diane asks. Her eyes follow Mark as he stops in front of the window. He's a silhouette against the bright backdrop of the midday light.

Mark chooses his words carefully but doesn't turn from the window, doesn't look at any of us as he speaks. "Brian used Reese as a way to get revenge on me."

"For what?" Diane asks.

He whirls around. "You really want to know?"

I stare down at my plate, mortified at what's happening.

"I fucked the girl he was in love with, so he did the same thing to me."

I feel sick at his words. These are things about sons no parent should ever know, and these are definitely things about *me* that I don't want Mark's parents to know.

"Language," Diane says sharply. She hasn't moved from her spot at Mark's kitchen table despite their heated words.

Mark rolls his eyes. "I'm sorry, mother, but you're in my house and I'm thirty-four-years-old. I think you know by now that I swear."

"Between your exhaustion and this girl, you're a different person, Mark," Diane says. Her voice is bitter and clearly speaks to the fact that she doesn't approve of the change.

He shakes his head. "No, I'm not. I'm the same Mark I've always been. I've just had a rough couple months." He turns back to the window, and we're all silent as we stare at his backside. "I was screwed over by my own brother and found out about it the same night Pops died. I've had to cancel shows, I've got a PR nightmare with this damn hospitalization, I've got Steve leaving the band, and everything with Reese is fucked up and I can't even get two seconds alone with her to tell her the things I need to say."

Wait a minute.

Steve's leaving the band?

seventeen

The three of us stare at the back of Mark while he continues to fix his gaze out the window. Silence blankets the room. It's not a soft and comforting silence like Mark and I have when it's just the two of us, but a loud and awkward silence that feels like it's seeping into my skin and infecting my body.

"We can take the hint, Mark," Paul says. Diane shoots him a dirty look and opens her mouth to say something, and I watch as Paul closes his eyes and shakes his head calmly at his wife. She glares at him but doesn't say anything else, and it marks the first time I've ever seen Diane back down.

I'm grateful to Paul as he stands and begins clearing away the remains of our lunch.

"I can take care of that," I say.

He nods once and presses his lips together into a thin smile. "Thank you, Reese. If there's anything you need, anything he needs," he jerks his thumb toward his son, "please give us a call."

"I appreciate that."

He helps his wife up from her chair. Diane walks over to Mark and laces her arms around him, hugging him from behind. "I'm sorry. Feel better."

He doesn't say anything to her.

"Bye," Paul says to me, and Diane ignores me as the two of them walk out the door.

We're engulfed in silence again once the door latches shut behind them, but Diane took the tension that hung in the air with her out the door.

Mark turns from the window and gazes at me from across the room. Our eyes meet, and all the passion and all the heat that was always there still passes between us. I'm cautious, though. He was just released from the hospital, but more than that, I don't even know if he wants me here.

"Steve's leaving the band?" I ask softly.

He nods as darkness spreads across his handsome face. "Not permanently."

"Why?"

He blows out a breath as he walks to his couch, and then he lies across the entire thing. I head toward the chair across from him, but he shakes his head and motions toward the cushion where his feet rest. I sit, and he rests his ankles in my lap. He's wearing jeans and he smells like the sterility that only comes from a hospital. He needs a shower and whatever it is he uses to smell like sandalwood. As I glance at his sock-clad feet in my lap, I can't help but realize that I haven't even had a proper hug from him yet. The closest contact we've had since I walked into his hospital room was this morning when he sat on the hospital bed and folded his arms around me, then later when he looped his arm around my waist as we got out of the car.

I need to feel him. I need to wrap my arms around him and breathe in his sandalwood. I need his mouth on mine and his cock sliding into me. I need his words and his breath and a future with him.

I realize all this as I stare at his feet.

He interrupts my thoughts. "He and Ang have struggled with getting pregnant for several years. She's pregnant and he wants time off to be with her through the pregnancy and birth."

"Why does he need to take time off?" My hands automatically start massaging his feet.

"She's high-risk and shouldn't travel. Our current tour ends in early December, but Keith has us running all over Europe starting in March." He lets out a moan as I knead the arch of his foot, and the sound sends a shot of desire straight through me.

I clear my throat. "Who's Keith?"

"Our booking agent."

"How do you feel about it?"

He purses his lips as his eyes go back to the window. "I can't be mad at Steve for wanting a life."

"But you are."

I feel his gaze on me, but I look down at his feet. "Before I met you, I never would've understood putting someone else before the band."

My eyes move to his. "And now you do?"

He lifts a shoulder. "I get it. He has a life outside Vail. We all do, but none of us have ever exercised our right to that life before. It took me a long time to come to terms with the idea that just because he's taking a hiatus doesn't mean we're breaking up. It doesn't mean it's over. He'll still meet us in LA for studio time, he just won't be touring with us."

I point out the obvious. "Between us, Mark, *you* are Vail."

He shakes his head. "We're a team of four."

"But you're the front man. People know you, recognize you."

"That's nice of you to say, but it's a team effort." His voice is adamant, and it tells me that the subject is closed.

"What are you guys going to do?"

He leans his head back on the couch and closes his eyes. "We have auditions set up in a few weeks around Lizzie's wedding when we have a tour break, but we might need to reschedule the canceled shows during those dates."

"How do you feel?" I ask.

"Tired."

I want to talk more, want to talk about *us* and want to hear the things he wants to say to me, but I don't want to push him.

"Go get some rest," I say softly.

He nods and stands. Before he goes to the bedroom, he helps me up. He doesn't let go of my hand when he asks, "When do you need to go back to Vegas?"

"I'm here as long as you need me."

His eyes burn into mine when he speaks next. "Quit your job. Stay with me. *Be* with me."

My jaw opens, but no words come out. Just some little squeaky sound. I don't know what to say. I can't just quit my job mid-school year to hop on tour with Vail because Mark wills it to be so.

Even if that's what I want.

He swallows thickly and squeezes my hand before he lets it go. He really does look exhausted. "Think about it. There's a key on the counter and Todd's number if you need to go anywhere. I don't know how long I'll sleep, but I want you to stay here with me, not at Lizzie's. I'd prefer in my bed, but if you're more comfortable in the guest room, stay there."

I nod, still at a loss for words, and he leans in, presses a gentle kiss to my cheek, then heads to his bedroom to get some rest.

* * *

I did some shopping on Michigan Avenue, and not just for me. I picked up a few groceries, and I realized as I was on my way to Lizzie's to grab my overnight bag that Mark's birthday is only a few days away. What do you get for the man who can buy anything he wants and has everything he needs?

I want to make the day special for him—he has a lot to celebrate this year.

His life, for one thing.

An idea formed in my mind of the one thing he *doesn't* have—the one thing he's never had. I'm bouncing with giddiness over my idea in the back of the Yukon on my way back to Mark's place when my phone starts ringing.

It's my department chair. I was just about to dig out the phone I've been ignoring all day to call her. I need to let her know I'm taking off the rest of the week, but she beat me to it.

"Hi Katherine," I answer.

"Reese, hello. How are you?"

"I'm good. I was just going to call you to let you know I need to take off the rest of the week."

"The rest of the week?" she repeats.

"I'm so sorry. I'm in Chicago helping someone who just got out of the hospital."

"I know. One of my sophomores showed me the photos on the internet this morning. You're the talk of the school."

My chest tightens. "What?"

"Mark Ashton's mystery woman finally identified," she says as if she's reading a headline.

"Excuse me?"

"Though I don't think Mr. Monroe's very happy. Don't get me wrong, he's thrilled with the money the private performance brought in for the auction, but he wants the focus to be on education. I'm sure you can understand that."

I'd forgotten about his donation to the school auction. I need to remember to ask him about that.

"I'm lost, Katherine. What are you talking about?"

"You haven't seen the articles online? The pictures of you getting out of the back of a big, black car with that singer?"

I blow out a breath. Of course—the paparazzi. My photo must be everywhere by now. Everyone was waiting with bated breath to know the very second Mark was released from the hospital, and I was there by his side as we walked into his building this morning.

God, was that only this morning? It feels like a lifetime ago.

"No, I haven't."

"What's he like?" she asks conspiratorially.

"He's the kindest person I've ever known," I say. I want to gush. I want to go on and on about how in love with him I am, but Katherine and I don't have that sort of relationship.

"He's not bad looking, that's for sure. How's he doing? Was it really exhaustion? I never believe that when I read about it in the magazines, you know?"

"He's doing great, just tired. Touring makes for long hours and not much sleep and it all just caught up with him." It's not a lie, exactly—it's true that touring is an exhausting activity. I don't answer the other part of her question.

"Anyway, Reese, Mr. Monroe just asked me to call you to let you know that we need to put you on a leave of absence."

"What?" I ask stupidly.

"The kids are all up in arms that their teacher is dating a celebrity, and not just any celebrity—one whose picture graces the lockers of half the girls in school. They'll want every detail about your personal life, and Mr. Monroe just doesn't feel that'll make for a very good learning environment."

"Curriculum always comes first. You haven't even given me a chance to prove that."

"It's been a circus here today and you're not even at school, dear. We've got concerned parents, distracted students, and you on the internet with a known playboy. Mr. Monroe did some research, Reese. He saw the types of photos that are out there of Mark Ashton, and he doesn't want that type of reputation associated with our staff."

"Oh my God, Katherine," I say as my heart starts racing. "Those are all old pictures put out by his publicist to build a certain image. That's not him."

"Unfortunately, it doesn't matter. The pictures of you with him say otherwise, and that makes you part of that image. We can't have that in an environment with children."

I suddenly want to scream, defend myself, do anything to prevent this conversation from where I'm suddenly sure it's going.

"I've filed paperwork with the district office for a leave of absence through December," she says. "More than likely it'll be through June, but we'll take one semester at a time. I'm working on a long-term substitute for your students."

Tears fill my eyes. "You're firing me?"

"No, you're not fired. It's a leave of absence. There's a difference. And if you disassociate yourself from him, certainly Mr. Monroe would be open to reinstating you to your position."

Anger shakes me to my core. "After he donated a performance worth four hundred thousand dollars to this school, you're telling me you'll take me back if we break up? Don't you see how twisted that is?"

"My hands are tied. I wish things were different. If you have a better solution, I'm all ears."

I too angry to think of a better solution. Instead, I end the call.

I just hung up on my department chair.

I toss my phone on the seat beside me as I realize what the fuck actually just happened.

I just lost my job. *Leave of absence.* Bullshit. It's as good as being fired.

And not just that. I just lost my job because of the same things Mark hates most about *his* job.

eighteen

I stand outside the door for a few moments as I collect myself. Mark needs me to be strong, and he doesn't need to know what just happened with Katherine. I'll tell him in time, but he doesn't need yet another burden placed on his shoulders.

"How do you feel?" I ask when I finally open the door and spot him on the couch as he watches some golf match. I swear, if I didn't know he was thirty-four, I'd think he's seventy.

I set my bags on the floor by the door as he stands from the couch and turns off the television.

His eyes heat as they fall upon me. "Better. Good enough for physical activity." He wiggles his eyebrows suggestively, but then he pauses for a beat as he studies me. "What's wrong?"

The dam bursts and tears pour out of me.

He rushes over to me. He pulls me into his arms, and it just makes me cry harder—the peace I feel here, the safety and the comfort, the love.

That glorious smell of sandalwood.

"What happened?" he asks as he holds me.

"I lost my job," I say through broken sobs.

"You were fired?"

"My principal put me on a leave of absence," I say shakily.

"What? Why?"

I draw in a deep breath to try to get through this conversation. "Students saw pictures of us."

"What pictures?"

"From this morning. Getting out of the car." I sniffle as the tears start to subside.

"Oh, fuck," he says. He pulls back and kisses my forehead.

"They said it was crazy at school today and everyone's talking about it and the focus needs to be on curriculum and not my circus of a life."

"I'm so sorry. I'll fix this. This is all my fault."

"No, it's not." I shake my head.

"How can you say that? You lost your job because you were with me. Fuck! And after I donated that performance." Anger flashes through his eyes.

"I meant to ask you about that," I say.

"What about it?"

"Why'd you do it?"

His eyes soften. "For you. But I never thought you being associated with me would cause you to lose your job."

"Don't talk like that. It's my choice to be here with you. I'd always choose you over some stupid job anyway."

He's quiet as he processes those words. "I love you," he says softly. He kisses the top of my head. "I still love you. I will *always* love you. Only ever you."

My eyes shine as I look into his. "I heard it on the radio."

"You did?"

I nod.

"What did you think?"

"I pulled over and cried in a parking lot. Why'd you do it solo?"

"Two reasons. One, Pen's been on my ass to release something solo. But more importantly, I wanted that song to be just mine. It's a song for us, not a Vail song."

I start to cry again at his words, and he lets me get it out for a few quiet beats as he hugs me closer. Eventually he says, "I'm so sorry. For everything." His hands smooth a path from my hair down my back and up again.

"Don't be sorry." I pull out of his hug and walk to the refrigerator. I grab us each a bottle of water.

"Let me make it up to you."

I shake my head. "You have nothing to make up. This was both of us fucking everything up."

"Speaking of fucking..." He grins slyly at me.

I can't help my laugh. "I don't know about that."

"You're gonna pretend you don't want it?"

"I have to. You're not ready for it." I take a seat at the kitchen table.

"Wanna bet?" He grabs what's clearly an erection tenting his shorts.

I ignore him. "Do you want something to eat?"

"No. You know what I want."

I raise a brow. "For dinner?"

"For any meal."

"Oh my God. You're impossible."

"No, I'm not." He shakes his head and gives me his best innocent puppy dog eyes, but I'm not buying it. "I need to test my physicality after everything I've been through."

"Play the sick card. Good way to get me to give in."

"If you don't want to give it to me, I can find—"

"Stop right there," I say, holding up a hand.

"So you're willing, then?"

I shake my head. "Eventually. We still have a lot to sort through, and the nurse said you need to take it easy for a few days."

He pulls out the chair next to me and sits. "I know. I'm teasing you. Mostly. I'm just ready for sex. With you."

"But you just said you could find someone else."

He purses his lips and shakes his head. "You cut me off. What I was going to say was that I could find a sock to blow it into."

My jaw drops. "Mark!" I scold.

He grins slyly. "I'm joking." His expression turns serious. "It's just been a while."

"How long?" I ask tentatively. I haven't had sex since the last time I was in this condo.

He looks away from me and out the window. "Since the morning you left."

"Really?"

He nods, and the last of my resolve weakens as everything inside me melts to a buttery, gooey mess.

"Why not?" My question comes out more cautious than I mean for it to.

"You know why not."

I touch his forearm, and his eyes fall on my fingertips. "I want to hear you say it."

"Because it was all meaningless bullshit." His green eyes finally lift to mine. "Everything else, I mean. I never felt anything real with any of them, and once I felt that with you, I couldn't go back."

Those pieces of my heart that were still fractured seem to find their home again at his words. Everything inside me warms. I lean forward and take his cheeks between my hands. The hair there is rough from days without shaving. The coarseness only serves to remind me that this is real. It's raw and real and *terrifying*, but every single moment with him has been.

That's who we are, isn't it? Why would it be any different now?

His eyes burn into mine, the green depths telling me this is what we both need. I lean forward and brush my lips softly against his. A low moan drops from him as he gives himself over to me, as he firms his lips and presses them to mine, and it ignites every ember of my quaking soul.

I want to deepen it, want to feel his tongue moving in my mouth, want to feel his hands illicitly moving everywhere, but neither of us moves for a few quiet beats. His kiss is familiar and perfect at the same time it's risky and petrifying. It's a promise for more between two people who are finally free to be together—if they want to. If they can make it work.

The sad reality hits me. I want this—of course I want this, and I think he wants this, too. But he's the touring front man of a multi-platinum band and I'm an unemployed teacher. How do two people from such different worlds find middle ground to cultivate a meaningful relationship?

I pull from our kiss first, and a disappointed grunt escapes him.

"How long would you have waited?" I ask.

"For what?" He looks confused.

"To have sex. How long would you have waited?"

"For sex with you? Forever." He gives me a cheesy grin.

"I'm serious."

He lifts a shoulder. "I don't know. Long enough for something meaningful to drift into my life again. Long enough to be sure I'd gotten over you before I moved on."

"And you didn't?"

He shakes his head and presses his lips together. He closes his eyes for a beat like he's in pain. When he opens them, they're a bright green and I feel like they're looking inside me. "No. I didn't even come close. How do you move on from the only one who has ever spoken to your soul?"

Tears prick behind my eyes at his words.

I get it. I get exactly what he means because I feel the same way. Each day has been an endless dredge of monotony.

"I have a question," Mark says.

I glance up at him and raise my brows.

"Who was the guy you were with on Friday?" His eyes darken as he asks, and my breath catches in my throat.

"That was Justin. My ex."

"Are you, uh...dating him?"

I huff out a laugh. "No."

"Then why did he have his arm around you?"

I furrow my brow as I think back. "He was trying to tell me something and I couldn't hear him. He was just leaning in closer."

He stares cautiously down at the table. "Do you want to be with him?"

I shake my head. "Not even a little. He's got a girlfriend and I've got..." I trail off. *Nothing.* I've got nothing, but now that I'm here, maybe all that can change.

"You've got?" he prompts.

I shake my head. "Nothing." I lower my voice. "I haven't been able to move on from what happened."

"Why not?"

"Same reason you didn't move on."

He nods in acknowledgment that the two of us were completely lost without the other one.

"Why'd you leave the show early?"

"I was devastated after I listened to you sing about how you hate me. Justin took Jill and me back to—"

Mark holds up his hand. "Wait a minute."

"What?"

"I'm sorry to interrupt, but those words weren't referring to you."

I raise both brows in surprise. "They weren't?"

He shakes his head. "I didn't know what love was until I met you. And while it's true I didn't know what hate was until you, either, it's not you I hate."

"Then who is it?"

"Isn't it obvious?"

I shake my head. "Clearly not."

His eyes go to the window again and he runs a hand over his hair and down his bristly cheek. "Brian."

"You hate your brother?"

He lifts a shoulder. "I don't know. I hate what he did. I hate that he kept us apart. I didn't truly understand that emotion until he tore us apart."

"Have you spoken to him?"

"Not since the day of the funeral. Finish your story about why you left the show."

He changes the subject so abruptly that I'm momentarily thrown off. I clear my throat and gather my thoughts. "He took me home, but Tess was banging some guy on the couch, so Jill and I went out for pancakes."

"What? Who's Tess?"

"Jill moved in with Becker and our lease was up, so I'm staying with my friend Tess. You met her that night you had the party when Lizzie was in town. And living with her isn't what I thought it would be."

"We'll fix that."

I don't know what he means by that, but my heart races as my head forms ideas. We're both quiet for a beat, and then he pulls my hand into his. He strokes the back of mine tenderly, and I stare down at his skin against mine—something I thought I'd never feel again.

"What did the last verse say?" I ask.

"The last verse of what?"

"'Until You.'"

He stands up, walks to the bedroom, and returns with a piece of paper. He sets it in front of me.

I read through the first two verses, the ones I heard on Friday.

And then my eyes fall on the third verse, and the hot tears that pricked behind my eyes a second ago fall in fat waves down my cheeks.

No matter what I do, I can't stop thinking about you
It's time to stop fighting it, Time to end this stupid shit
I need to find you, need to say, I want you back, it starts today.

"You want me back?"

His eyes shine as he watches my tears fall. He flicks one away with a rough fingertip. "Yeah. I want you back. I just don't know how to get you back. I want these last twenty-four hours to change things, but I don't know if it does."

"Of course it does." My voice is a passionate and desperate plea.

He lifts a shoulder. "I'm on tour. We've cancelled shows because of my stupidity. I've let everyone down, and not just the band. Fans. My family. You. And the root of everything stems from how fucking dumb I was to let you walk out of my life."

"I never went anywhere," I whisper.

"Yeah, you did," he says. "You went back to your life and walked out of mine, and I didn't fight for you. That's what I do, Reese. I push people away. I fuck up everything good."

"Why?"

His brows dart down. "Why?" he repeats. "That's not what I expected you to say."

I lift a shoulder. "What did you expect?"

"I thought you'd say something about how that's not true. Something to make me feel better."

I press my lips together. "Don't fish for compliments, Mark. Not with me. I need your honesty, always."

He glances away from me.

"So why do you fuck everything up by pushing everyone away?"

His gaze goes to the window, but I grab his jaw and force his eyes back to mine. I don't know where this strong version of me is coming from, but I like her.

"Fear?" He says it like a question, and I nod in encouragement.

"What are you scared of?" I drop my fingers from his jaw.

"Losing you."

"You lost me. How'd it feel?"

"It sucked."

I chuckle. "It wasn't exactly a picnic for me, either."

"I do it to make it on my terms. I do it so I can brace for impact. If I fuck it up before it ever gets off the ground, I have less to lose."

His eyes burn into mine, and they're so intense that this time *I* am the one who has to look away. My eyes are drawn to the windows.

"Is that why you lied about the girl at Sevens?" My voice is soft.

"Yeah."

I glance over at him, and he's looking down at the table. I don't say anything.

"I'm sorry," he says. He's so earnest that I can't help but believe him. "I shouldn't have led you to believe it happened that night. That picture was from a long time ago and I'm pretty sure my brother had a hand in releasing it anyway."

"Seriously?"

He nods.

"So where do we go from here?" I ask.

"To the bedroom?"

I smack him in the arm, and he grins at me.

"I meant to go to bed. My nap wasn't long enough, and I really do need some rest."

I laugh. "I'll make us some dinner, and then bed sounds perfect." I stand to move toward the kitchen to figure out something for dinner, but his soft voice stops me.

"Come back to me," he says softly. I turn around to look at him. "I can't live this life anymore without you."

His eyes burn into mine, betraying the passion he feels for me despite his quiet tone.

Was there ever really a question?

"On one condition," I say.

"Anything," he says. His eyes are hopeful, and I can't help but wonder what's going through his head at my words. I could ask for anything in the world, and from the sincerity in his eyes, I'm sure he'd give it to me. I run through a mental catalog of everything I'd never ask him for—leaving Vail like Angelique did to Steve, cutting off contact with his mother like he did with his brother, money or luxuries or vacations or cars.

I don't want any of that, though. Vail makes him happy. His family is his family, and even though I hate what Brian did, he's the one who called me to let me know Mark needed me. While he's the reason we were torn apart, he's also the reason I'm standing in Mark's kitchen right now, the reason I'll be staying the night here, the reason we moved past the *clean break* I thought I needed so we could be together. They'll find their way back to each other because they're brothers.

"I want you to vow to me right here and right now that you'll stop the self-destruction." My voice wavers. "The world almost lost you way too early because of your own stupidity, and I won't stand by and watch you do that ever again."

He closes his eyes and nods. "I promise." He opens his eyes and slides out of his chair. He pulls me into his arms as he makes his vow. "Why would I do something so stupid when I have everything I need right here?" He tightens his arms around my waist, and I hug him close to me.

"I'm done being stupid," he says. "I'm done having pissing matches with Ethan, done letting him try to prove he can make it all go away when the only person who really can is you. I won't lose you again."

Tears heat behind my eyes as I squeeze him closer. I won't lose him again, either.

"Destiny," he whispers. He takes my hand to pull me with him. Neither of us is wearing shoes as he leads me up the stairs to the roof.

It looks different than it did the last time I was here, probably because Brian isn't lying helpless on the ground. I glance at the spot where I tried to help him, but it's clean. No trace remains of what happened except the scars on our hearts.

Mark's eyes darken as he watches me look around, and then he says, "I need you to promise me something, too."

Anything. "What?"

"I need you to tell me that you want me for *me*."

I gaze up into the green depths of his eyes for a beat. "I want you for you. I'm honestly a little offended that you'd even think that."

He shakes his head when he hears the defense in my voice. "I mean I don't want this to be some twisted attempt to save me. I don't need saving. I just need you."

I step into his arms where I belong. "I'll save you if you need saving. I'll hold your hand if you're in a hospital bed or taking the stage or on a rooftop in Chicago. I'll be by your side for whatever you need whether we're living in a penthouse suite or renting a tiny shack on the side of the road. It doesn't matter as long as I have you breathing next to me."

His mouth crashes down to mine. We had that little kiss yesterday, but this is something different. This is fiery passion, this is bottled up need detonating between us.

This is love.

It's a battle of tongues and clashing of teeth, but he still holds onto his signature sensual steam as he brutalizes my mouth with his. The desire that pools in my abdomen presses a fierce ache between my legs.

He still needs healing. He needs time and rest. No physical activities for a few days.

These reminders dart through my head, but when his tongue brushes mine in that way only he does, the words are obliterated and lost in a sea of achy need.

He holds me so tightly against him that I can't move. All I can do is breathe him in and tighten my arms around him. Our bodies are so close we're melding together as one. All that separates us is the fabric of our clothes.

I'm about to tear off his shirt and toss it over the railing despite my good sense when he slows and ultimately stops the kiss.

I break away breathlessly, and he's panting, too. He sits on the couch.

"Are you okay?" I ask softly.

He stares into the darkness of night lit only by a few lights left on in the building across from us. "Yeah. Just got a little dizzy for a second."

His kisses do the same thing to me.

I sit next to him and rest my palm on his thigh. I want him—need him and crave him—but his health has to come first.

"You were just released from the hospital, Mark. You're recovering and you need rest. Let's get you to bed."

He rolls his eyes. "It wasn't that big of a deal. It's like a bad hangover that lasts a few days."

I narrow my eyes at him. "A bad hangover? It was an *overdose*, Mark."

"I know I got lucky. The doctors called it an overdose because that's the medical term. But I'm fine."

"Prove it. Go see a doctor, get medically cleared, and then we'll talk."

He blows out a breath, but he knows I'm right. Sex will have to wait another day.

nineteen

I wake up in a tangle of blankets and tattooed arms. Mark's leg is tossed over mine, and he sleeps soundly beside me. It must be early; the room is dim as light is just starting to peek through the side of the blinds.

It was early last night when we crawled into bed, just after he vowed to stop his destructive path and kissed me like he needed my breath to survive.

As I stare at him beside me, I'm struck at how surreal all this is. I've known an image of this man for ten years, but the reality is so different from what I imagined. So much better.

I've never known love like this. I've never wanted to be close to someone just to hold him. I've never wanted to give up everything I know so I could be by his side through every trial life throws at us.

I have no idea where we go from here. It's not like I have a job waiting for me back in Las Vegas. I don't have a home, not really. I miss that feeling of home—that feeling of having a place to go where you belong no matter what.

I untangle myself from the man I love and make my way toward the bathroom.

"Morning," Mark says softly when I emerge after a shower. He flipped the sheet off his body. He slept in just a pair of shorts, and my mouth waters as I look at the strong chest and stomach inviting me back to bed.

"Sorry for waking you," I say. "How are you feeling today?"

"Good enough for sex." He says it hopefully, and I laugh.

"Let's give it an hour and see how you're doing."

He rolls his eyes and huffs, and I giggle again. I sit on the edge of the bed.

"I want to go home," I say. I have an ulterior motive for my words.

"Me too."

I glance around. "You are home."

He shakes his head. "Home is wherever you are."

My heart swells. "How did I manage to get so lucky with you?"

He lifts a shoulder and his abdominal muscles ripple. "That whole thing about rock stars making fantasies come true." He chuckles as he catches me staring at his abs. "See something you like?" he asks. He grabs the bulge in his shorts just under those abs, and a pang of desire bolts through me.

"I see a lot of things I like, and right now I'm trying to remember exactly what the doctor said about how long you have to wait for sex."

"I'm fine, babe."

"I need breakfast first."

He laughs. "Fine. But then your ass is mine."

He makes me his ninja scrambled eggs then heads to the shower while I clean up our breakfast dishes. I call Jill and fill her in on the latest events of my life, and then I call Rachel and tell her everything, too. They're both thrilled that Mark and I found our way back to each other.

I'm about to call my mom when he comes out of the bedroom with an overnight bag. Aviator sunglasses are perched on his nose and he's wearing jeans and a black t-shirt. I want to strip him naked and have my way with him in the middle of his kitchen. Immediately.

"I have a surprise for you," he says, pulling off the sunglasses. "Get your bags."

"Where are you taking me?"

His eyes sparkle as he stalks toward me. He pulls me into him with one arm around my waist and presses a soft kiss to my lips. "If I told you, it wouldn't be a surprise. Now go," he says, smacking my ass to get me in motion.

I giggle as I scurry to the bedroom to pack up my stuff. Less than an hour later, Todd drops Vinny and the two of us off at Chicago's Midway International Airport and we board Mark's private jet.

After we take off, Mark leads me back to the part of the plane I've never seen—the part separated from the rest of the cabin by a door. He opens the door and leads me into a bedroom complete with a queen size bed, a dresser that appears to be bolted to the floor, and a huge television.

"I figured you'd force me to rest, so let's rest as we travel to our destination and then we have the whole day ahead of us."

A few hours later, we move to the seats up front and buckle up for landing. Mark grins at me as we look out the window together and the familiar hotels of the Las Vegas Strip come into view.

"Home?" I ask as tears fill my eyes.

"You said you wanted to go home."

"And you make fantasies come true."

He lifts a shoulder. "Just yours."

"Why?" I ask.

He gazes tenderly down at me. "Because I love you."

I answer with a kiss, and then it's time to get off the plane and into the back of another Yukon. "Sal!" I greet Mark's driver with enthusiasm, and he nods and smiles at me.

Minutes later, we're pulling up at the Mandarin Oriental. So many memories, both good and bad, attack me as we get out of the car and head toward the elevators. A few paparazzi are standing out front and snap our picture. Mark's wearing his aviators and I keep my head down, but it doesn't matter anymore.

The world can finally see us together.

Once we're inside Mark's familiar penthouse, I say, "Thank you for bringing me back to Vegas, Mark, but this isn't my home."

"I think we should talk about that," he says.

A tingle of nerves shoots down my spine. "About what?" I ask cautiously.

"You mentioned where you live doesn't feel like home. If you're looking for a new place to live, I would love if that new place was my place." He sweeps his arms out. "Here. With me. And on the road, and in LA and Chicago and New York."

I can't help the smile that plays at my lips. "Are you asking me to move in with you?"

He nods with confidence as if he knows my answer before I even say it, but then he starts rambling nervously. "I can get your stuff from Tess's place over here within an hour. I want you in my bed with me, in my sheets, by my side. If you're not ready for that, you can stay in one of the other rooms and we can just be roommates for a while and learn to live together, learn to be a couple. But if you're ready, I'm ready. I want this. I want you and I want to rise up against this world with only you."

I can't help my grin. "Okay."

He grabs me up in his arms and twirls us around before he covers my mouth with his.

"Really?" he asks. His smile is so wide that his eyes have little crinkles at the corners. He looks at me with boyish elation, and if not for the tattoos snaking along his arms and the dark scruff lining his jaw, I might mistake him for someone else.

I nod. Of course I'd say yes. It's not just convenient, it's also the only place I want to be. "I don't have anywhere else to go, but I also don't have anywhere else I'd *rather* go."

"You'll go on the road with me, too?" He looks so hopeful and so excited that even if I wanted to, I have no idea how I'd ever say no.

"I'll try it. But we need to find something for me to do on the road. I can't just be Mark's girl, you know what I mean?"

"I'll talk to Pen. We'll figure something out."

He crushes his mouth to mine, and despite the force, he's gentle and slow with me. His kisses invoke a vow as he tells me that it'll only ever be me, just like the song says. I kiss him back in response, making sure he understands it's the same for me.

Despite the very different worlds we come from, I have the sudden inclination that when we face life together, we'll be able to overcome anything that's thrown our way.

He breaks our kiss but continues to hold me in his arms. "Let me make a few calls to get your stuff here," he says.

"I never unpacked most of my stuff, but I'd prefer to box up what I did unpack myself."

He nods. "Let's head over there now, then. We can fuck on that couch where you saw her banging someone else."

I crinkle my nose. "I'd rather have our reunion sex somewhere sexier than that. And cleaner."

He laughs.

"I have a surprise for you, too." I head over and grab one of the bags I got on Michigan Avenue and hold it out for him. "This is for you. Happy early birthday. Before you open them, though, I need to know one thing."

"What?" He eyes the bags with the excitement of a child, and I smile.

"How are you feeling?"

"A little tired after flying even though we slept on the plane, but I'd say I'm running at about ninety-five percent."

"Do you need to rest?"

He shakes his head.

"Are you up for a little adventure?" I ask.

He nods.

"Do you promise you'll tell me if you're feeling even a little bit too worn down?"

"I promise," he says, holding up one hand.

I gesture to the bag, and he starts taking items out of it.

"A long-sleeve red shirt with a dog on it, a pair of khaki shorts, and a Cardinals hat?" He avoids actually wrinkling his nose at the thought of wearing a football hat featuring a team other than his precious Bears. "This is my birthday present?"

I nod and grin. "Do you have flip flops?"

"I'm a man. Men don't wear flip flops."

I roll my eyes. "Fine. Casual shoes aside from your black Nikes?"

He nods. "Why?"

I shake my head. "You'll see. Open this one." I hand him another bag, and he pulls out the contents.

"A horse mask and a cow mask?"

I giggle. "Open the last bag."

He pulls out a bunch of papers I printed online and starts reading the places on each as he flips through them. "Caesar's Casino, Fashion Square Mall, Ziplining Downtown, Hike Red Rock Canyon, Outback Steakhouse. Denny's?" He glances up at me halfway through the stack. "What is all this?"

I lift my chin proudly. "It's your birthday present. Your gift from me."

He looks confused. "Well, you nailed it. These are definitely things I don't have. Um...thanks?"

I step over and tap the papers in his hands, a smile playing at my lips. "You pick whatever you want to do. I'm giving you the gift of a day of normal."

His eyes soften and his jaw slackens a bit in surprise as he stares at me. "No one's ever given that to me." His voice is soft and full of wonder.

"We'll wear sunglasses and hats. I got the masks in case you wanted to be silly. You'll look like a tourist in khaki shorts. No one's *ever* seen the famous rock star in khaki shorts and a Cardinal's hat. Ditch the black Nikes and wear something different. And the sleeves on the shirt will cover your very recognizable tattoos."

He tosses the papers on the kitchen table next to the rest of his gifts. He closes the gap between us and hooks his arm around my waist. He hauls me against him, his eyes intense and hot. He leans his face down to mine, and butterflies take flight in my belly as tingles burst through my chest. My heart races and my breathing labors. It's the same crazy, intense effect he has on me every single time he holds me close, but this time, his eyes glow with adoration.

"This is the best present anyone has ever given me," he says, and for some reason, a sense of some future déjà vu overcomes me when he says that, a sense that someday I'll give him an even better gift when I hand him a child born from our love.

I shake off the thought. We're barely even officially back together. I don't know what's going to happen next, but I feel like life has handed us the worst already. What lies ahead can't be any worse than the last six weeks without him.

He brushes his lips to mine, slow and sensual, a total tease before he backs away and blows out a sigh. He makes a show of adjusting himself.

I don't want him to stop. I never want him to stop.

But he's only at ninety-five percent, and just like Penny said about his voice the other day, I want him at a hundred percent for me, too.

"What do you want to do first?" I ask.

"I want to take a walk down the Strip."

"Are you sure?" I ask.

He nods. "Yep."

"Then you better get changed."

Before I even finish my sentence, he's tearing off his t-shirt and pulling on the long-sleeve shirt I bought for him. He lowers his running shorts, which I discover he's wearing nothing underneath, and I can't help but stare hungrily at his semi-hard dick that looks very lonely all the way over there.

"Um, Reese?" Mark says. I snap out of my trance and look at his face. He points to his eyes. "My eyes are up here."

I giggle and blush then walk over to the window to look out over the view of the Strip—a view that's played over and over in my mind and now belongs to me, too.

* * *

"I thought the best grand slam ever was when I went to a Cubs game back in the mid-nineties and saw one in person." He takes a bite of his pancakes and shakes his head. "I might've been wrong."

We left the horse and cow masks back at Mark's place when we walked out. When Vinny met us in the hallway outside Mark's front door and asked where we were going, Mark simply told him, "For a walk."

I laughed the whole way down the elevator. Mark Ashton doesn't ever just go *for a walk*.

Vinny followed a few paces behind us so he didn't draw attention to us. Even he's wearing a hat, and so far, no one has recognized Mark. It's a little trickier now that he's taken off his sunglasses since we're inside, but we're in a corner booth and he's facing the back wall. The chances of someone recognizing him are slim, and our waitress is about forty or fifty years older than Vail's key demographic.

"Mine's pretty good, too," I say. I take a bite of bacon and close my eyes as I savor the sweet, sweet taste of the pure, fatty pleasure.

"Stop it," Mark says, his voice a mix of commanding and joking.

"Stop what?"

"That little moan you just did." He shifts on his side of the booth.

"What little moan?"

"The bacon-moan."

"Sorry," I say, but it doesn't come out very apologetically when I laugh. "It's good."

"You've never moaned like that for me."

I raise a brow. "If you tasted like bacon, I might."

He glares at me, and I giggle again.

"I've got some sausage for you," he says.

I shake my head. "There you go again."

"What?" He's the picture of innocence.

"Just when I think you're this cool rock god even on our day of normal, you say something like that and knock yourself down a few pegs."

He takes a sip of coffee to hide his smile. "So how long am I supposed to wait for sex?" he asks.

I purse my lips. "You're impossible."

"I know, but I'm also adorable. So...?"

"The nurse said to give it a few days. It all depends on how you feel."

"I feel good enough for a normal day." He nods his head resolutely. "Which includes sex."

"You've mentioned that," I say dryly. I take another bite of bacon, careful not to bacon-moan this time.

"If I could walk all the way to Denny's, don't you think I could also have sex?"

I consider his point. "Probably not both on the same day."

"We better get a ride back then."

I laugh, partly because he's being silly, but also partly because he looks ridiculous in his bright red shirt and matching bright red hat. You'd think it would draw attention to him, but it doesn't. It works as he blends in with the other tourists.

"Trust me, Mark. I want to, too. But I think we need to make sure you're ready."

He nods. "I do have something sort of serious I want to talk about."

My brows draw down. "What?"

He clears his throat and avoids eye contact. "That night on the roof, the one with Brian..."

"Yeah?"

"He, um...mentioned something about going in bare." He pushes his eggs around his plate with his fork. "What are your thoughts on that?"

I'm confused. "About Brian going in bare?"

"No," he says. He finally looks up at me. "About *me* going in bare."

My cheeks redden. "Oh." It's all I can manage to say.

"Forget it," he mutters.

"No, it's...um...it's just..."

He shakes his head. "It's okay. Someday, maybe. Forget I mentioned it."

"No, I mean yes. I—yes. That would be nice."

"Nice?"

I giggle nervously. "You know what I mean. I'm just..." I don't know how to say what scares me the most.

"What?"

I draw in a deep breath. "I know your reputation, Mark."

"I've never done the bare thing."

"Okay, but you...wait. What?" I stare at him incredulously. "You haven't?"

He shakes his head.

Holy shit.

I could be another first for him.

"Okay, but things happen. Condoms break. I just—"

He cuts me off. "They ran my bloodwork when I was in the hospital. We're good to go."

"Oh. Wow." It's all I can manage to say.

"Are you on birth control?"

I nod.

"I assumed so since you let someone else in bare."

I narrow my eyes at him. "Is that what this is about?"

"What?"

I feel a bit of understanding clash with a bit of anger. "You wanting to get in there without anything between us. Is it to stake some claim?"

He shakes his head. "No." He's adamant. "It has nothing to do with that. It's about wanting nothing between us except skin. It's about needing the type of connection with you that I've never shared with anybody before you. It's about love and respect and understanding. But if it's not something you're ready for, that's okay. I won't push you. I'll wait until you're ready."

"I'm ready."

He glances around us. "Like right now?"

I giggle. "Well, yeah. But no."

"I can think of somewhere nicer, or at least more private, than a corner booth at Denny's for you."

"Like where?" I ask. "The bathroom?"

His eyes light up. "Ooh, good idea."

I roll my eyes. "Absolutely not. Bareback happens in beds. Well, the first time at least."

"Boring," he mutters.

"Excuse me?"

"Beds are for boredom." He raises a brow at me like it's a challenge.

"Beds are for backs," I counter, folding my arms across my chest and raising a brow back at him.

"Beds are for burnouts."

"Beds are for banging."

"You win," he says. "Let's go bang on my bed."

"I'm still eating."

"Oh yeah, baby. Eat more bacon while I watch." He makes a show of pretending to beat off under the table, and I can't help but crack up.

After I pay cash for our dinner despite Mark's insistence that I let him treat, we walk back down the Strip. We stop at a hole in the wall casino and play some five-dollar blackjack—where we both lose—and we stop at another hotel to walk the mall and shop. Neither of us buys anything, but we window shop and hold hands and point out things we think the other one would like.

We get frozen yogurt for dessert and he feeds me a spoonful of his. We laugh and people-watch, walk and talk, and it feels like something a normal couple would do out on the Strip on a normal afternoon that shifts into evening.

"This is the best early-birthday ever," he says as I feed him a brownie bite from my frozen yogurt. His sentiment warms my heart.

We walk through the doors of the Mandarin a little after five. It's been a fun few hours together, and I don't think either of us wants it to end...but it has to—for now, at least. Mark needs a little downtime.

"Do I get a full twenty-four hours of normal?" he asks.

"You can have whatever you want, but I want you to take an hour and rest while I go to Tess's and get some of my stuff."

"I'll come with you."

On our way to my place, he calls his doctor. He's able to get a quick appointment, so we swing by the office, where he's medically cleared for any and all physical activities.

Sal drives and Vinny rides up front just like always. I slide my key into the door a little before six, and Tess is sitting at the kitchen table with papers spread out in front of her as she grades a stack of essays.

"Hey, Reese," she says, glancing up at me and back down at her papers.

I watch as she does a double take, her eyes focusing on Mark.

"Oh my God," she says. She drops her pen and her eyes widen. "Oh my God. Mark Ashton is in my apartment! Mark Ashton is in my fucking apartment!" She smooths a nervous hand over her hair and stands.

I giggle. "I have some news." I glance over at Mark. "Well, *we* have some news."

"She's moving in with me," Mark says.

I elbow him in the ribs, and he grunts.

"Oh my God. My best friend is moving in with a rock star?" Tess is shrieking and I'm a little worried she might start hyperventilating.

"We're just here to get some of my things."

"Can I do anything?" she asks. "Can I get you anything?"

This is literally the most hospitable she's been since I moved in with her.

"We're fine," I say. "Oh, and there's one more thing. You might already know through the grapevine, but Katherine and Mr. Monroe put me on a leave of absence. So I won't be coming back to school." My eyes find Mark's. "Well, unless we break up."

Mark rolls his eyes and shakes his head. "She won't be coming back to school."

I laugh, and we leave a very surprised Tess near the kitchen table. I pack the things I care the most about, and then we head out of the bedroom to take a load down to the Yukon. I'm struck with complete awe as I watch the backside of Mark Ashton move through a tiny apartment as he carries a box of my things. He brings the box to the car, but before I head out the door, I stop and say goodbye to my short-lived roommate.

"Thanks for letting me crash here a while," I say, giving her a hug.

"Sure." She squeezes back, and I feel for the first time that despite everything, we can still be friends.

"I'll send someone around for the rest of my stuff if that's okay."

She nods. "Whatever you need."

"Hey, take care of yourself, okay? If you ever need to talk, you know my number."

She smiles. "Enjoy the rock star."

I grin. "Oh, I will. And you be good to Jason. Either get over your fears or cut him loose."

Her eyes wander down to a spot on the floor, and she nods. I give her another hug, and then I make my way toward the rock star waiting at the car for me.

twenty

We step onto the elevator at the Mandarin, and Mark twists his Cardinals ball cap around so the bill is in back. He hauls me over to him by my waist as soon as the doors are fully closed. We left the boxes in the car for Vinny and Sal to carry up, so it's just us here.

His breath is warm peppermint against my mouth, he smells of sweet sandalwood, and I'm reminded of *us*. Everything in the world turns right side up, just as it should be.

He kisses me softly, sensually. Both of our mouths are closed, yet the kiss is full of passionate abandon that presses a needy ache in my core. The elevator slows to a stop and it also means the end of our embrace. He leans his forehead down to mine. "Only ever you," he says quietly, and a shudder of desire leaps in my stomach.

He pulls away and I follow him into his penthouse.

"Now what?" I ask.

"Sex."

I laugh. "You've mentioned that once or twice."

"I feel good, Reese. I'm ready."

"I know you are. And I am, too." I wander toward the windows. "But we have a lot of little details to think about."

"Like what?"

"I know I've already jumped the gun and agreed to move in with you, but we've barely even dated. We've spent all of five days together. How do I date a rock star?"

He stands next to me by the windows but doesn't touch me. "I'm just a regular guy, babe."

I laugh. "No you aren't."

"Fine. A regular guy who's maybe better looking than the average guy."

"Maybe?" I gesture toward him. "Definitely."

"What else?"

I narrow my eyes at him. "Are you fishing for compliments again?"

He lifts a shoulder. "No. I just want to know what makes you think I'm any different from any other guy you've dated."

My heart stutters a little at that thought considering his *brother* happens to be another guy I dated.

"You've got talent, fame, fortune, looks, and," I glance down at his stomach, "Jesus Christ, those abs."

He laughs.

"Seriously, though. You've got millions of adoring fans. You're gone all the time on tour. You can't just take me to dinner and a movie like a normal guy could."

He nods, conceding. "I could rent out an entire theater for you and have dinner brought in."

I laugh. "I know you could. But that's not what this is about."

"I get it. Being with me...it won't ever be normal." He turns his gaze back out the window. "That birthday present you gave me was the best gift anyone has ever given me, and it took that to show me something I'd been blind to."

I so badly want him to turn toward me, to let me see his eyes. Instead, he's focused on the people walking the sidewalks forty-seven stories below us.

"What?" I ask.

He turns toward me. "I may not be a regular guy. Our relationship may never be ordinary. But I've never known what normal was until you showed me. That's what you are for me."

"Normal?" My brows furrow down low and my voice comes out with a bitter twist to it. I'm not sure why, but I feel a little insulted by his words. I don't want to be *normal* for him. I want to be special.

He nods. "You provide order in my disorderly mind. You provide logic in an irrational world. You give me a sense of home just in being who you are. Routine. Structure. Tradition." He finally turns his head to look at me, and the genuine affection I see there blows me away. "I've never had those things, Reese, but now that I've had you back with me for a few days, I realize how much I need them." He closes the gap between us and pulls me into his arms. "Need *you*."

His eyes focus on mine, hot and full of hope, lust, love, and pure *fight*, and that's the moment I know I'll do whatever it takes to make this work with him.

"I want you naked in my bedroom," he says. "I want to show you what you mean to me, and I want to do it this time knowing it's not to say goodbye."

* * *

After everything we've been through, it's finally time. This is how he asked for me, so this is how I stand. I'm completely naked, my back against the windows overlooking Las Vegas Boulevard in his bedroom. It's just after nine at night. The sun has gone down, but the city is enveloped in lights on the other side of the window.

I twitch nervously as I wait for him. A lot rides on this moment. We've spent the day together doing *normal* things after the very unusual activity of flying on a private jet from Chicago to Vegas. Having a conversation, eating at Denny's, stopping at the doctor, running to my place...all things that normal couples might do even though we're far from normal.

And now, this. Another thing normal couples do, but somehow it will be extraordinary as well.

When the door finally opens and he emerges from his bathroom, he's wearing just a pair of jeans. I want to kiss him and worship him. I want to run my tongue along every single centimeter of his body.

I take a tentative step toward him, but he holds up his hand as if to say I should stop and stay where I am. I freeze and wait for him.

He strides across the room toward me leisurely, as if a mountain of pressure doesn't hang on this exchange between us, as if we haven't both built this up in our minds to be something bigger and better than it was before.

But he's the one who can ever maintain his cool, the one who can put on the act like he's in total control. He *is* in total control, always disciplined despite his flaws and the occasional mistakes that he assured me won't happen again.

His fingertips skim my jaw. I close my eyes and let out a soft sigh.

"God, Reese," he whispers, the strain evident even in his quiet voice. I open my eyes to him just like I've opened my heart to him—only him. I stare into his green depths, and I see everything I need to see. Most importantly, I see a future for us.

His mouth moves down to mine and he kisses me slowly, his tongue circling mine. He rocks his hips against me, the full hardness of his erection through his jeans grinding against my most sensitive skin.

He massages my breasts in his palms before he runs his hands along the tips, grabbing them in a decadent twist that causes me to cry out with pleasure before he lets go. He soothes the ache with the pad of his finger before repeating the process over again, every twist and tug sending a delicious ache through to my core.

I'm panting, breathless, and he's only kissed me and touched my breasts. As his tongue continues to brush against mine, his fingers trail down. He slides a finger through my slickness, grunting when he feels how wet I am. He pulls his finger to the front to massage my clit before gliding back through. He doesn't push it in, and my needy body aches for him.

I grind my hips down on his hand as I search for some sweet relief, but he drops his hand instead of giving me more. I moan in deprived disappointment, and I feel his grin against my own lips.

"You're impatient tonight," he murmurs. "Guess I better get moving."

I chuckle, but truth be told, I don't want him to go any faster. I want this to last forever.

He grabs me up into his arms and carries me to the bed. He sets me down softly then he gets rid of his jeans and climbs over me. He hovers above me for one sweet moment before he lowers his head to kiss me. Our bodies aren't connected yet apart from our mouths, and I feel my release sneaking up on me. The buildup not just from today but from the all the days since the last time we've done this come between us. I push it all to the past as I focus on him and me and this connection we share.

"Are you sure about this?" he asks. I know he's talking about sex without a condom, that conversation we had at Denny's.

I nod. I've never been so sure about anything in my life, but the emotions in the back of my throat prevent me from saying that.

"Thank fuck because I've never been so hard in my life," he says, reminding me how long it's been for him, too.

He glides his swollen head through me, and I jerk forward in anticipation. He strokes himself a few times against my clit, and the illicit feeling of skin on skin pushes me over the edge. I'm about to come when he glides down and slips inside me.

The raw feeling is unbelievably smooth. He pumps his hips back and forth, driving into me and pushing me closer to release.

"God, I missed you so much," he murmurs. His voice is laced with all the same emotions I feel.

He grunts at the same time a low moan rumbles out of my chest, a sound I can't control even if I wanted to. I gasp and pant for him as I claw my nails into his back and dig my heels into his ass, anything to draw any part of him closer to any part of me. I push my hips up to meet his thrusts. He's in control and disciplined when I just want him to hammer away at me, to push me into the headboard and into next week, but I know he won't because he wants to draw this out. It must be beyond painful for him, but if he goes fast, we both lose. Instead, he's slow and deliberate, each powerful thrust punctuated by a low groan.

"It's so fucking good, Reese," he says. "I could fuck you like this forever."

His words are broken by the grunts of his thrusts. He groans out a loud growl when I scratch my nails across his skin, but my body is acting totally on instinct at this point. I try to respond, try to tell him I want that, too, but all that comes out is some broken moan followed by a series of gasps.

He starts to drive in a little faster, pushing me closer and closer to my release. His thumb comes between us to stroke against my clit, and that's when I lose all control. I yell out his name or something like it along with a series of words that might sound something like *Oh-fuck-fuck-Mark-shit-fuck-oh-oh-oh*, and he matches my sounds with a series of his own *oh-fuck-fuck-Reese-shit-fuck-oh-oh-oh*s. He thrusts in a little more forcefully a few times before he stops and holds himself still as he spills into me. The feeling pushes me right into my own orgasm, my body pulsing around him and contracting, prolonging his release. We match each other's moans, an erotic soundtrack of pleasure playing in my ears as we both lose ourselves in the carnal perfection of the other.

He hovers over me for a beat, his eyes hot on mine, before he pulls out of me and collapses beside me, tossing one arm over my chest.

"Holy fuck, Reese," he mutters after a few quiet minutes pass between us. He doesn't move, and his voice is muffled by my shoulder. "That was..."

He doesn't have the words. The man who writes words for millions of people to hear every single day doesn't have the words.

I supply the phrase he's looking for. "Even better than bacon."

He laughs. "Wow, that means a lot. You even bacon-moaned for me."

"Damn right I did. But I think you have it backwards."

"I do?" He sits up to rest on his elbow.

I nod. "I Mark-moaned for bacon once."

He laughs and covers my mouth with his.

twenty-one

Since the doctor cleared Mark earlier than we expected, the tour resumes earlier than we expected, too. We had less than twenty-four hours for me to pack anything I want to bring on the road with me for the next month. Mark says I can come and go as I please, but I'm ready for this change. We'll land in Chicago at the end of October for a tour break surrounding Lizzie's wedding, and then we'll resume the tour through the beginning of December.

Everything has happened so quickly that I haven't even called my parents to fill them in. Between having a lot of sex with Mark since we had to make up for lost time and trying to fit everything I need to take with me for the next month into one wardrobe cart, I haven't had a spare minute.

But now it's time. Mark is in his office video chatting with his tour manager, Penny, and the rest of the guys as they reschedule dates. I dial my mom's number nervously. I haven't even told her that I was put on a leave of absence from work. I'm not exactly sure how this conversation's going to go.

"Hi, honey," she answers. She doesn't even let me get a word in before she starts talking. "Good timing on the call because your sister and Ben are here. We're talking wedding plans!"

She's giddy with excitement and I have a feeling my news will have to wait.

"Tell Rachel to call me on video chat so we can see each other," I say. "Then I can help plan, too."

"Oh, great idea! We'll call you right back." She hangs up, and my phone dings a minute later with an incoming call.

I wander over to the corner of the family room and sit in Mark's comfy recliner as I pick up the call. "Hey everyone!"

"We picked a date!" Rachel says. "Remember how I said we either want to elope tomorrow or wait a while?"

"Yes..." I say.

"Well, it's neither. There's this gorgeous place in Sedona that had an opening in July, so we nabbed it."

"So ten-ish months?" I ask.

"Exactly ten months from today!"

I think about that for a minute, wondering where in the world we'll be in the next ten months—wondering how much will change in that span of time. "I'm so happy for you, Rach." I grin at my sister. Ben waves behind her. "You too, Ben!" I watch as my mom and dad move in behind them and we all wave at each other for a few seconds. I giggle and look awkwardly at myself then tuck a strand of hair behind my ear.

"Where are you?" Rachel asks, squinting to look around me.

I notice for the first time that there's a guitar hanging on the wall directly behind me.

"Um, that's sort of what I called to chat about. I'm glad you're all there."

"What's going on, honey?" my mom asks, yelling like I can't hear her.

I giggle. "Well, Mark and I are back together."

"Oh my God!" Rachel squeals. My parents exchange a look, and my mom's cheeks turn pink.

"It's a long story, but I'm also going to go out on the road with the band for the rest of their tour." It sounds absolutely ridiculous when I say it out loud. This is my fantasy. This can't be reality.

But it is.

I pinch my leg to remind myself that it's real.

"What?" my mom whispers incredulously just as Rachel shrieks.

"What about school?" my dad asks, always the first to point out the logistics.

"Well, some pictures turned up linking Mark with me, and my principal didn't like having one of his teachers associated with someone who has his reputation."

"Your dad isn't sure he likes it, either," my dad says.

I shake my head. "Dad, you were the one who took us to all the Vail shows when we were teenagers. Remember?"

Mark saunters into the room. He's across from me, in my line of sight but not in the camera's view for my family to see him through the phone. He grins at me.

"How could I forget?" he says. "But you're my daughter. I've heard what they say about him."

Mark's eyes darken as he realizes we're talking about him. He strides over toward me.

"What they say is inaccurate," I say. "And I'm in love with him."

Mark steps behind me and leans down so he's in the camera shot. He waves and kisses the top of my head. "I'm in love with her, too. Hi, I'm Mark."

"Holy shit!" my sister squeals.

My mom gasps, and my dad and Ben's eyes both widen.

"My publicist posts what she wants. Most of it's not true, and I'll be talking to her now that I'm with your daughter. I never cared about my image until I had someone in my life who I care about more than myself."

My heart soars. I know his words are exactly what my parents need to hear.

"We'll be in the southwest at the beginning of November," Mark says. "I'd love to swing a trip to Phoenix and introduce myself."

They're all silent. I think they're in shock, and I giggle. "He's just a regular guy, you guys," I say. "Dad, I caught him watching the Golf channel the other day. You two can talk golf."

Mark shrugs and grins, and my sister's jaw drops at his panty-dropping smile.

I giggle.

"Nice to meet you, Mark," my dad finally says.

Mark's phone starts ringing. "You, too. I'm so sorry, but I have to take this call."

He answers it and strolls out of the room, and my family stares at me with their wide eyes.

"So that's Mark..." I say.

"Reese, he's very handsome," my mom says. My dad elbows her and I giggle.

"What about work?" my dad asks, and I realize I didn't finish answering his question earlier.

"My principal put me on a leave of absence after he saw the photos. I don't want to work in a place that reacts that way, anyway, and Mark asked if I'd go on tour with him."

My dad's apparently the only one who can find his voice. "So that's it?"

"Yeah. That's it. We leave tomorrow and I'd love your support." I'm about to add that I'm going with him whether or not they agree, but my mom comes through for me.

"Of course you have our support. Always, baby girl."

"I love you guys," I say.

"We love you, too," my mom says. My dad nods, and my sister still looks shocked that she just saw Mark Ashton behind me. "We just worry about you. You better check in all the time and let us know where you are, and you better be safe." She rambles some more, and then we chat a little about wedding plans and what life on the road will be like, and I'm thrilled that I'll be leaving tomorrow with my family's blessings.

Later, Mark and I luxuriate in each other with more sex—this time slow and sensual. He pulls out of me at the last second and jerks himself onto my stomach. I watch his face twist as he comes onto me, claiming me as his, marking his territory, sexy and masculine and hotter than anything I've ever experienced in my life.

He sits back on his heels for a few beats as we both fight to catch our breath. He eyes the mess he made on me.

"Sorry," he says, his voice smug.

"No you're not."

He laughs and stands. "No, you're right. I'm not." He disappears for less than a minute then returns with a wet washcloth to clean me up. Even *that* turns me on, his warm hands running gently across my body as he takes care of me.

"What will tomorrow look like?" I ask. We're flying to Atlanta in the morning for a show tomorrow night.

He drops the washcloth and climbs into bed beside me. "Well, usually bus call is two A.M., which means we all need to be back at the buses and ready to travel to the next city overnight. That's what the crew will be doing."

"How many buses are there?"

"Three. Ethan and I share one and James and Steve share one. Then there's a crew bus."

"You ride apart?"

"When we night travel, yeah. But when we day travel, lots of times we go together. My bus has a little spot where we can remix and write. But then you're stuck on a bus with somewhere between five and ten other people for a lot of hours."

"Who?"

He tosses an arm across my stomach. "It depends. Usually Ethan, Steve, James and me, sometimes Morgan and

Angelique. Sometimes Vick or Penny depending where we are. Sometimes Keith. Sometimes Ethan has someone with him." He omits the fact that in the past, he might've had someone with him, too. "Plus our driver."

"Do you usually sleep on the bus?" I want every single detail about life on the road, and I can't believe I'll get to experience it starting tomorrow.

"If it's an overnight trip, yes. But if we're day driving, sometimes we'll hammer out lyrics. Other times we just watch movies or play video games or poker to pass the time. The only bus rule is don't be a dick."

I giggle. "I promise not to be a dick."

"So much shit can come up when you're in close quarters and you're stressed because of schedule fuck-ups or whatever. It's important to remember we're all in it together, not against each other."

"Is anyone ever a dick?"

"Ethan pretty much always. That's why Steve and James got their own bus." Mark flips over to turn off the light then snuggles closer into my naked side. "I'm excited for you to come with me."

"I am, too," I say softly. Excited and nervous.

* * *

The air is humid in Georgia even though we've slipped from summer to fall. The car that carried us from the airport to the Verizon Amphitheater pulls behind the venue next to three large tour buses a little after three in the afternoon. Mark gets out of the car first and helps me out. We walk over to one of the buses, and a driver stands outside it.

Mark nods to the driver then introduces me. We step onto the bus, which is complete with couches, comfy chairs, a table, a refrigerator, and a large television. He closes the curtain separating the forward section from the bunks. The bus driver must've brewed coffee because I spot a pot full on the counter. Mark helps himself to a cup and grabs one for me, too.

"I'll give you the full tour later," he says quietly, nodding toward the curtain. "Ethan's sleeping back there. If the curtain is closed, that's the quiet voice signal."

We sit on the couch, Mark's arm around my shoulders and my hand on his thigh. Vick hops onto the bus next, a large soda in her hand. She's a bubbly ball of energy who barely seems able to maintain her quiet. "How are you feeling?" she asks, plopping next to him.

"One hundred percent." He tightens his arm around me. "Thanks to her."

Vick smiles. "Good work, Reese. Glad to see you back here."

I give Vick a warm smile back just as a blonde beauty I've never seen before steps onto the bus. Her wide blue eyes complete with fake lashes fall onto the man sitting beside me and she flips her long, wavy, perfect hair over her shoulder.

"Mark!" she yells with glee, obviously not understanding the rule about being quiet when the curtain is closed. She flings herself at him and perches on his lap despite the close quarters of Vick on one side of him and me on the other. She's actually sitting on my hand since it was on Mark's leg, and I can feel her skin through her ripped jeans. The heel of one of her black hooker boots bumps my leg but she doesn't care as she kisses him on the cheek. "How are you feeling?"

Clearly she also doesn't know the rule about not being a dick.

He doesn't answer her question. "What are you doing here, Zoey?" Mark asks, not removing his arm from around my shoulder as he uses his other hand to force her off his lap.

She grins widely, ignoring the fact that he just pushed her off his lap. "Came to see my favorite boys!"

Mark blows out a breath and looks at Vick.

"Zoey, can you give us a few minutes?" Vick asks.

"Of course!" She flings open the curtain and disappears behind it.

I clear my throat. "Um, who's that?"

"That's Zoey," Mark says.

"Yeah, I got that," I say dryly.

"She and Mark only dated for a little while," Vick says.

I turn an angry gaze on Mark.

"How long is *a little while*?" I ask.

He glares at Vick then blows out a breath. "On and off for a year or two."

"*A year or two*?" I screech. I thought he said he'd never been in love, but he had a long-term girlfriend who looks like *that*?

"It was a long time ago, and it was all physical," he says. "I never wanted more than that."

That doesn't make it any better, not with the mental image of her perfect little body riding on top of *my* man and not when I'm left to assume that she *did* want more. I shake my head in disgust, but I force myself to be understanding. He can't help that girls throw themselves at him and he can't help that he has a history. This is just a tiny preview of what I can expect going forward.

I've been part of his professional life for all of five minutes and this is already harder than I thought it would be.

"Why does she think she can just go wherever she wants on your bus?"

He grits his teeth together then blows out a sigh. "She's Ethan's sister. She lives here in Atlanta."

The picture clarifies. So this is why Ethan hates me so much. I thought it had more to do with the fact that I was taking his wingman away from him. I figured he saw me as the girl taking away his best friend.

It could be more than that, though—it could be that Ethan assumed his sister and his best friend would end up together, that Mark would always be a part of Ethan's family.

What Ethan might not understand, though, is that Mark and Zoey don't need to be together for that feeling of family. What Vail has *is* family.

Even as that thought enters my mind, I remember what Mark told me about Steve. Their family is breaking apart, and Mark committing to me must make Ethan feel like he's losing two brothers.

I don't have much time to stew on that because Ethan and Zoey appear from behind the curtain just as Steve and Angelique board the bus followed by Morgan and James. Vick looks annoyed since she didn't even get a full minute alone with Mark to talk about whatever she wanted to talk about.

"He's back," James says, and Mark stands and slaps each guy on the back in that bro-hug thing guys do. He gives both Morgan and Angelique a small kiss on the cheek. Morgan grabs me up into a big hug, and Angelique hangs back, looking bitter and annoyed—things I now understand much more about than I did when I first met her.

Zoey skips off the bus. Steve, James, and Ethan talk with Vick about something on one end of the bus while I stand with Mark, Morgan, and Angelique.

"How are you feeling?" Mark asks Angelique.

"Tired," she says. "You?"

Mark shrugs. "Back to good."

"Good. We missed you." Her words are laden with a deeper undertone, and I get the feeling she doesn't just mean over the past couple days. The real Mark was buried inside himself, missing in action for the past six weeks. It's probably the nicest thing I've ever heard come out of her mouth. She looks at me and purses her lips. "You're sticking around this time?"

I glance over at Mark. He's smiling down at me with love shining in his eyes. I nod at Angelique. "That's the plan."

"Does she know?" Angelique asks Mark quietly.

He nods. "She knows everything."

She shakes her head and lets out a small chuckle. "I wouldn't have believed it if I didn't see it with my own eyes. He told you private band stuff, so you must mean a lot to him. Congratulations to you both, and I'm sorry I was an epic cunt when we first met."

I laugh. "That's a little harsh."

"All right. A really big bitch." She smiles wryly. "Between being the reason behind Steve's sabbatical and feeling the need to protect my Vail boys on top of pregnancy hormones, I didn't give you a chance and I'm sorry for that."

"Forgotten. It's in the past," I say.

"Thanks for bringing him back to us," she says softly.

I give her a hug because I'm suddenly too choked up to say anything.

While the men and Vick video chat with Penny and Keith to work on their schedule, I sit on the couch and watch Mark. He's in his element as he takes the lead, and I wonder what he was like while we were apart, if he was still the leader or if he took a backseat. Since Angelique thanked me for bringing him back, I have a feeling it was the latter. He's truly back now, though, and he's better and stronger than ever.

The boys have their soundcheck, a fan meet and greet, and pre-show rituals while I hang with Morgan and Angelique on the bus. It's our little home away from home, and I've even gotten the full tour now. The back of the bus has an actual bedroom complete with a king-size bed that Mark already claimed for us. I even changed the sheets while he was off at his meet and greet since only God knows what went down on those sheets while Mark was away.

"Those weeks you two were apart were hell on all of us," Morgan says as I grab a bottle of water from the fridge. I plop on the couch next to her. "Well, maybe except Ethan."

"Why?" I ask.

"When he wasn't being an asshole to everyone, he was moody and unpredictable," Morgan says. "He wasn't himself."

"He was unfocused and unhinged," Angelique adds from a recliner across from us. Her hands rest protectively over her abdomen.

"And now?" I ask.

"Even just in the few phone conversations he's had with Steve since you came back, he's himself again," Angelique says.

Morgan turns back and smiles warmly at me. "A better version of himself."

I wonder what that means, how I make him a better version of himself, but I bask in their words. I bask in this moment—I'm really, actually a part of this group, the *significant others* club. I'm part of the in crowd with the wives of the members of Vail.

Five months ago, I was a fan with a fantasy. And now...this is my life.

I blow out a breath of disbelief as we relax in the air-conditioned cab of a tour bus behind a amphitheater and Morgan and Angelique fill me in on everything I missed.

I debate asking them about Zoey, but I trust Mark, so I leave it alone. Soon we're heading back to the dressing room for our pre-show shot.

I hold my tiny shot glass filled with Jägermeister up next to Morgan's. Angelique shoots me a grin from across our tight circle as she holds up a shot glass filled with water. My hand is steady this time as I wait for the rhyme I know the words to.

"To show six eighty-eight," Mark says. "Good pitches, no hitches, no forgets."

Everyone, including me this time, chimes in together with, "No regrets!"

I swallow down the black licoricey-tasting liquid and set my glass on the table with everyone else. We're all standing, and as soon as Mark drops his glass on the table, he pulls me into him. He presses his lips gently to mine.

"Wish me luck," he says just like he said last time as he leans his forehead to mine.

I say the same thing I said last time, too. "You? Nah, you don't need it."

He laughs at our new little ritual. "Nah, you're probably right," he says, and we both laugh.

He kisses me again. "Watch me from side stage?"

"Nowhere else I'd rather be."

Vick leads the boys out of the dressing room and toward the stage. Mark clutches my hand as we follow. I glance over at him. His gaze is focused ahead of us, intense as he prepares to take the stage in front of a sold-out crowd at a venue that fits twelve thousand people. He must feel my eyes on him because he looks over at me.

Vick picks up the pace because it's show time. The boys don't have time to waste, but Mark spares a second to kiss me once more.

It's a slow, sensual, tender kiss. I hear a drum somewhere in my periphery. I hear a bass guitar join in. But Mark is still kissing me.

He pulls away and his eyes meet mine for one intense second, and then he runs to the stage just in time to join the music with the first line of their opening song. His eyes meet mine more than once as he works the stage and does what he does best, and I find my feelings growing inexplicably stronger with every note he sings.

***

"What the fuck, Pen?"

Mark is pissed. He should be celebrating his big return to the stage after a drug overdose, but instead he's yelling at his publicist on a video chat a little after one in the morning.

"People needed to know you're okay," she says.

"I'm capable of telling people I'm okay, and I have a girlfriend now. Stop tweeting pictures of me with other women."

She sighs. "I'm sorry. I didn't think you'd even notice."

"That's not an excuse. I know you think I can't handle my own social media, but I don't want Reese getting the wrong idea. Or my fans, for that matter. I'm with someone, and it's serious. I don't want people thinking I'm out with a different woman every night anymore. It's not fair to her or them."

"You're right, and I apologize to you both."

I wave at her from behind Mark to indicate that I'm not mad. He's more upset about it than I am, to be honest. He's lying on the bed with his iPad and I'm sitting behind him, propped against the headboard. The bed is just like the ones in all three of his homes that I've slept in.

"Don't do it again and we won't have a problem. But I want my social media control back." His voice is so firm that his next words strike me as a silly contradiction considering he just went on and on about how he's capable of handling his own social media. "What's my Twitter password?"

I giggle.

"It's the same as your Facebook one. You realize you're paying me to do this and it'll take a big load off my plate, don't you? You want to handle all the social for Vail or just the Mark Ashton accounts?"

"You can keep Vail. I just want mine."

"I need better images for the Vail platforms," Penny says. "I've had to dig deep into the archives or pay local photographers. A personal, inside look will sell you better. Vick sends me some pictures here and there, but she's too busy working her ass off for you to take pictures. People want venue views, backstage tours, sneak peeks into soundchecks, that kind of thing."

Mark glances at me with his brows raised.

"What?" I ask.

"Would you want to do it?" he asks.

My brows draw down in confusion. "Handle your social media?"

"Handle Vail's social media. And mine. I'll pay you."

"Oh my God, Mark, that's perfect," Penny says. "She's right there with you. She can provide backstage access. She's got a degree in English so she can handle writing captions. She can be like my on the road Vail assistant."

I think about it for all of two seconds. Taking pictures of Mark Ashton and telling the world how awesome he is sounds perfect to me. I'd do that for free. "Absolutely."

Mark grins at me and leans over to kiss me.

Penny's voice interrupts us. "Hey, you two. At least turn off video chat if you're gonna pull that shit."

Mark pulls back and raises his brows. "Hmm. Video. An interesting idea, Pen."

I roll my eyes and giggle. "Better not do it on my phone. Wouldn't want to accidentally post the wrong thing to your Instagram."

Penny looks at us in horror. "Maybe this is a bad idea."

"I'll be careful," I say. I know what a big responsibility this is—it's probably nearly a fulltime job in itself, and I can't imagine the astronomical number of fans Vail has across all the social media platforms, not including Mark's personal accounts.

"You two get some sleep or whatever it is you do and I'll be in touch with passwords and instructions tomorrow," Penny says.

We hang up, and I can't help my excitement at the prospect of an actual job for me on the road with Mark Ashton.

twenty-two

Tonight, Vail will be performing their last show before the tour break for Lizzie's wedding. In the last few weeks, I've been thrust headfirst into a world I know nothing about. Including Atlanta, I've been on tour for sixteen shows over twenty-six days. Typically, the boys perform two or three nights in a row then get a night or two off. On the nights off, we get to sleep in a hotel—a luxury I appreciate more than I ever thought possible.

I *love* touring the country with Vail. It hasn't been all sunshine and red wine; we've had some growing pains and fights. It took me a good two weeks to even be able to fall asleep on a bed in the back of a moving vehicle. I felt awkward the first time we had sex back there when I knew Ethan was just on the other side of the door with a woman of his own. And last night, we got into an epic fight when I went to the hotel ahead of him while he took care of a few things with the guys. He called me to check in and hung up on me when some woman whose voice I didn't recognize called his name.

I refused to answer when he called back, but later I found out that one of the crew guys had fallen off some scaffolding and broke a few ribs. It was my fault we got into a fight over it. Mark yelled at me not to shut him out ever again, and I yelled at him never to hang up on me again, and then we made up in the sweetest, most aggressive way.

Despite the minimal struggles, it's been one adventure after another. We're seeing parts of the country I've never seen before. We cuddle in bed on the bus as we look out the window at the landscape passing us by. He's more than I ever expected him to be. He puts me first, worries about my needs and comfort over his own. But that's something Lizzie told me—that he puts everyone else first.

So I put him first. He won't do it, but someone should.

I've even gotten used to the women who embarrass themselves in the presence of a man who has a girlfriend. They grab his ass, pull his arm toward them, fling their arms around him—and worse. Much, much worse.

He's always gracious, but I can tell it wears on him—not because he doesn't revel in the attention, but because he hates what it does to me.

The darkest cloud is Ethan. I keep waiting for a breakthrough, but he hasn't warmed up to me at all. His sister only attended that one show in Atlanta, though I admit I was worried she'd go on the road with us for a few stops, and I wasn't sure how I was going to handle that.

Ethan tends to bring a different woman back to the bus every night. When the bus is rocking, we hang on the other one. Mark and I don't talk about it, but I often wonder if that's how he acted, too, before I came along.

"After the show tonight, I promised Ethan I'd do an appearance with him. Is that okay with you?" Mark asks me a few minutes before he needs to leave the bus and head backstage for pre-game—a ritual I still know nothing about. I'm sitting on the bed on the bus with my new work laptop on my lap as I read through the comments on the video clip I posted earlier from today's soundcheck.

"Of course," I say. "You don't need to ask me. It's part of your job. But before you go, I need some pictures. Maybe of both of you."

He leans down to kiss me, and the butterflies that flutter around my belly tell me that even though some time has passed, his kiss will always be special. "You didn't let me finish." His breath is hot and minty against my lips.

I raise a brow. "Go on."

"The last time we did an appearance, I landed in the hospital for a couple days."

"You vowed you wouldn't self-destruct," I remind him. "So as long as you keep your word, we're good."

"I'm a man of my word. You know that."

I nod. "I trust you."

The adoration in his eyes as he smiles down at me still sends a shock of giddiness through my system. "Good. And speaking of words..." He trails off and opens one of the dresser drawers. He flips through a stack of papers, finds the one he's looking for, and closes the drawer. "I wrote a new song." He folds the paper nervously in half and sets it on top of the dresser.

"When?"

"I started it the morning you left me in Chicago, and I finished it yesterday. I want you to be the first to see the words."

"Before Ethan?" I ask. Ethan may be a dick, but he's also an amazing lyricist and Mark's right-hand man when it comes to songwriting.

He nods. "It's a song for you, and I'm planning to use it on my solo album."

"Album?"

He grins. "Pen booked me studio time in February. It's after the US tour and before Europe. I've already got a drummer and a bassist lined up."

"Are you sure you want a solo album?"

He lifts a shoulder. "I never thought about it before, but between Steve doing something for himself and you stepping into my life, I'm inspired to do something for me."

I set my laptop beside me and stand to pull him into a hug. "I'm so excited for you."

He presses a kiss to my neck. "I need you there every step of the way. I want to run lyrics by you, I want you to listen to the riffs. I want your opinion.

"Me?" I ask. "But I'm a fan. I'll love anything you do."

He runs a fingertip along my jaw. "That may be true, but I also believe you want to see me succeed as much as I do. That's what a real partner is, and that's what you've become for me."

I lift my chin and press my lips to his, amazed that I'm somehow the one he chose to become his partner.

"Open it when I go," he says softly, nodding with his head toward the piece of paper on the dresser. He kisses me once more then disappears through the bedroom door to head backstage.

I wander over to the dresser and pick up the folded piece of paper. I raise it to my nose and breathe it in, catching the faintest hint of sandalwood as I do.

And then I open it. Before I read any of it, I glance down the page. Some words are crossed out and others are scratched out. The page is a mess, but I can easily read what he wants me to read. I focus on the title at the top of the page, and my breath catches in my throat.

Clean Break.

I close my eyes for a beat as I feel those two words wash over me—words I said to him when I left him in Chicago, when I told him that was what I needed from him.

And then I read the lyrics.

I would've given it all up for you
When we parted ways up on that roof
They say I'm stupid to pine for you
I'll write another song to show the proof

We said our goodbyes
But they were full of lies
You wanted a clean break
But it was only heartbreak

I haven't touched another woman
Since the morning when you left my bed
I don't want any other woman
Can't get you the fuck out of my head

We said our goodbyes
But they were full of lies
You wanted a clean break
But it was only heartbreak

Too terrified to lose you
Started my own self-destruction
I lost myself on the road
Without you there is no sun

We finally said hello again
Back in my arms where you belong
We got our clean break at last
When I left behind my sordid past

When I'm done reading the words, tears are streaming down my cheeks. He's given up so much to be with me, just like I have for him. And that's what a partnership is.

He's right. We needed a clean break, but I didn't realize that it wasn't a break from each other. It was Mark who needed to leave some things in the past so we could find a future together.

I want to get him alone before the show so I can tell him how much his words meant to me. We have a new beginning together, and I want to celebrate that. But it'll have to wait until later.

His eyes find mine when I walk into the room after their pre-game. His are heated and full of all the same emotions I just read on a piece of paper. We do our Jägermeister toast and then Vick leads us all to the stage.

"Wish me luck," Mark says, pulling me into his arms. His mouth is inches from mine.

"You? Nah, you don't need it." I'm breathless at his proximity.

He's smiling when he kisses me. "Nah, you're probably right."

He runs to the stage after one last kiss, and I take my spot beside Angelique on the side of the stage. Morgan is on her other side, and the three of us hold hands. I squeeze Angelique's hand in mine. Tonight is the last time she'll be with us for a while. She won't be coming back after the tour break, and the boys will be auditioning someone who can temporarily take Steve's place while we're in Chicago. Mark seems to know everyone in the music industry and has worked with tons of prominent musicians. His approved list of who could potentially temporarily replace someone as irreplaceable as Steve is short.

I'm glad it's dark on the side of the stage, because the emotions I felt after reading the "Clean Break" lyrics are still lurking as a lump settles in my throat.

I've watched this same performance sixteen times in the last twenty-six days, and it never gets old. I take some pictures and a little video footage for social media posting, but mostly I just watch.

I watch as Mark owns the stage. I watch as he runs past me then stops and backs up to plant a sweaty kiss on my mouth before he grabs a clean shirt from Vick for the second half of their set. I gaze at the perfect abdomen that'll be all mine later as he rips off the sweaty shirt and pulls on the new one. I watch as he works the crowd with that rock star magic he has and as they take their final bow after their encore.

I wish I could say that then he's mine, but he has an appearance to do. He takes a quick shower and I head back to the bus.

He pops in with a quick goodbye kiss while I lay across the couch, and then he's off to hang with his best friend while I get the bus to myself.

Except I don't.

A knock at the bus door forces me up from my comfortable position. Morgan and Angelique stand just outside the door, and Morgan holds two glasses of wine. "Girls' night?" she asks, holding one of the glasses up to me.

"Hell yes," I say, and they climb the stairs.

Angelique pulls up a romantic comedy on Netflix and we all settle into various comfortable seats on the bus. This really is like a home on the road, like my best friends have come over to spend some quality time together.

As Morgan plays idly with my hair and we sip wine, I realize how true that is. While I do miss Jill and she'll always be my best friend, we text every day and talk a few times a week. She's about the only thing I miss from my old life in Las Vegas, and I think it's because I've found a niche for myself in this new life.

twenty-three

Lizzie and Dave's rehearsal and wedding are both located at the Adler Planetarium deep in the heart of Chicago. The views are spectacular, but I can't take my eyes off my date. It's rare to see Mark Ashton wearing anything other than jeans and a t-shirt, but tonight he's wearing gray pants and a long-sleeve black shirt. He looks dressy even though he still maintains his casual appearance, and I can't wait to see him in his tuxedo tomorrow. I think I might die from lust.

"Reese!" Lizzie throws her arms around my neck with exuberance after she hugs her brother hello. "I'm so happy you're here." She's glowing, an excited bride ready to get married tomorrow. Tonight's rehearsal dinner also marks the first night I'll be in the same room as Mark and Brian since that night on the roof.

I'm expecting the boys to act like adults for their sister, though a tiny part of me is also expecting fireworks of epic proportions.

I don't know whether Brian will have a date for the wedding. I typically see wedding dates as pretty serious, especially when it's your sister getting married, but if I were in his shoes, I wouldn't want to show up alone.

Lizzie breaks into my thoughts as she leans in close and whispers, "Thank you. You fixed him. He's never looked better."

A little heat forms behind my eyes as I pull out of our hug. "Are you ready?" I ask her.

She grins and grabs Dave's hand in hers. "A little late if I'm not!"

Mark slides his arm around my waist. "Can we do anything?" he asks her.

She shakes her head as she points her finger at Mark. "You've done enough."

He grins. "You got it?"

She presses her lips together like she's trying not to cry, and then she nods. "We got it."

"Got what?" I ask stupidly.

Mark waves his hand in the air like it's nothing. "Just a final little deposit to help cover some of the last-minute expenses."

"Little?" Lizzie asks, shaking her head. She looks at me. "It was enough to cover the entire wedding, honeymoon, and down payment on a new house."

"How big is that fucking house if it's only enough to cover the down payment?" Mark asks. He elbows Lizzie in the ribs good-naturedly, and she jumps while I giggle.

Diane and Paul are talking to Gram and another couple around their age when Mark walks up and taps his mom on the shoulder. She turns around and throws herself into his arms.

"Oh, Mark! You look great!"

"You're beautiful, Mom," he says. He hugs his dad next. "I'd like to introduce you both to my girlfriend, Reese," he says.

Diane narrows her eyes. "We've met."

"Clean slate," he says in a tone that makes it sound as if he's reminding her of a conversation they've had before.

Diane blows out a breath. "Nice to meet you," she says, sticking out her hand to me.

I smile awkwardly. "You, too."

Gram hugs me next, and as she does, I say quietly to her, "Thank you for your note. Your words stuck with me in all the dark days."

She pats my back lovingly. "Thank you for all you are for him."

That damn heat presses behind my eyes again while Paul hugs me then introduces me to his brother and sister-in-law.

We're looking across the water at the distinctive Chicago skyline as the last embers of light fade to the blackness of night. Mark's arms are secured around my waist when I feel the hairs on the back of my neck stand at attention.

Mark looks over my shoulder and stiffens. He lets out a low curse. The air shifts, and I know immediately that Brian is here.

I turn to look, too, and I see that he did bring a date.

Kelsey, his modelesque bitch of a secretary, has her arm hooked through his as they make their way toward Lizzie and Dave. They make an attractive couple—her with her long legs looking like she just stepped off the runway and him in that damn suit and tie that gets me every time—but they also make me want to barf.

Anger bubbles inside me. I knew from the beginning that he and his secretary had a thing. I don't really care anymore that he was screwing her while he came between Mark and me. I don't care that he forced us apart while he made me believe we had a future together. It would be hypocritical of me to even think about that anymore after Mark and I got together behind his back.

I don't even care that she's the one who got stuck with him. They can have each other.

But I do care that he's flaunting her here tonight. After everything the three of us went through, after his phony apologies, he has the nerve to bring this bitch to his *sister's wedding*. He knew I'd be here tonight, and he knew his brother's arm would be around me. To parade around with Kelsey is just straight up disrespectful after he banged her on the side while he tore Mark and me apart.

Fuck him, the witch by his side, and the broom they flew in on.

I pull out of Mark's arms and begin to storm over to him. Mark grabs my elbow and attempts to pull me back, but I'm on a mission that's not to be stopped.

The patio where the dinner is located has started to fill with people I don't know—relatives, bridesmaids, groomsmen, dates. Music plays from some hidden speakers, a quiet and tranquil instrumental piece. The din of voices rises and falls over the music, a crescendo of music in its own right.

Most people here already know Mark and aren't star struck by him, but the people who've never met him stop and stare as we hurry past.

I storm over to Brian with Mark hot on my heels. I wait until he's done introducing his *date* to his sister. When he turns around, all bets are off. I don't know what I'm going to do, but it's not going to be pretty.

"Mark, Reese. Lovely to see you. Reese, I believe you've met my date, Kelsey." The cocky grin is back on his lips, and I need it gone.

Something comes over me in that moment, some primal need to protect both Mark and myself. It's animalistic, a real fight or flight moment, and my body screams to fight. This asshole gets it all—the successful business that he built because of his brother, the pretty girl who doesn't care that he was with me while he was fucking her on the side, the love of a mother who turns a blind eye to the awful things her son does.

It's not right.

I slap him across the face with a loud crack that seems to echo into the night.

Kelsey gasps and the smug smile slips from Brian's lips as every person on the patio seems to go quiet at the same time.

"Fuck you." My words are a quiet hiss.

Mark pulls my stinging slapping hand in his and starts to pull me away. "Not here," he says sharply.

He leads me inside just as we hear someone outside say something that causes the group of people gathered to laugh. The noise resumes, but it's muffled from in here.

"What the hell was that?" Mark asks.

My sensibilities seem to come back to me as the red that took over my vision fades back to normal colors. "I don't know. I'm sorry."

"This is Lizzie's weekend," he says. His voice is hard and direct, and I hate that he's using that tone with me. "I won't allow anything to ruin that, least of all Brian."

I nod. "I need to apologize to Lizzie."

He nods. "That would be nice." One side of his mouth tips up in a smile. "You cracked him good."

"Think I left fingerprints?"

He chuckles. "I hope so. Fucker had it coming."

"I thought if anyone was going to hit Brian this weekend, it'd be you."

He lifts a brow and nods. "Me too." He focuses his gaze out the window, and I follow his line of sight. Brian's having a conversation with one of the groomsmen, and Kelsey stands by his side looking a little lost. "But I made a promise to myself that I'd move forward. What he did doesn't matter anymore."

"Of course it does."

He shakes his head and turns his gaze back on me. "I went through some pretty dark days without you, Reese. But I've got you back now. The darkness is gone. Part of me wants to say fuck the road that got us here, but the other part of me recognizes that Brian played a pretty big part in the two of us finding our way back to each other. In the end, that's all that matters."

I run my fingertips along his jaw, the bristles there awakening the desire that's always inside me for this man. Love blooms in my chest for him and it rolls over me like a wave. I never knew I could love someone this hard, this much, this strongly.

"You're a better man than he is," I say softly. "You're kind and forgiving. He doesn't deserve that."

Mark pulls me close by my hips. "You're right, he doesn't. But you and I deserve happiness, and if that means forgiving Brian so we can push that shit to the past, then let's do it."

"Oh God," I say, covering my face with my hands.

"What?" He pulls at my hands, and his eyes are full of concern as he gazes down at me.

"Did your mom see me hit Brian?"

Mark laughs, and it's not a small chuckle or manly little snicker. It's a full-on, hysterical laugh that infects me, too, as I start to giggle.

"Can we talk?" The serious voice interrupts our laughter. Mark looks up and I whip around.

Brian and Kelsey stand just a few feet away from us, and Brian looks earnest as he waits for our reply to his question.

"About what?" Mark asks icily—a contrast to the words he just spoke to me.

"I don't want to fight with either of you." His voice carries a hint of desperation.

"Then why did you bring her as your date?" I ask, nodding at Kelsey.

"Because she's my girlfriend."

"Can I ask you a question?" I ask Kelsey.

She nods. She looks one part terrified of me and one part awestruck to be in Mark's presence as she clings to Brian's side.

"Why would you want to be with someone like him? Someone who was screwing you on the side when he was trying to seduce me away from his brother?"

Kelsey looks surprised. She glances over at Brian, and he nods as if to tell her it's okay to speak. I'm not sure I care for that dynamic, but I'm also not sure it's any of my business. Maybe I'm misreading the situation.

She clears her throat. "We didn't get together until recently."

Brian nods. "It's true. There was always an intense attraction between us, but we never did anything behind your back." Their eyes lock, and a genuine affection passes between them. "I knew what I was doing to you was wrong, but I wasn't going to drag Kelsey into it."

"You're so full of shit," I say.

They both look shocked, but frankly, they deserve one another.

"Reese, stop." Mark slings an arm around my shoulder and pulls me close. "Let them have each other." He presses his lips to my temple and then looks at his brother. "Thank you for calling Reese." He doesn't say anything else, but both Brian and I know he means when he was in the hospital.

Brian nods. "We all have Kelsey to thank for that. She knows everything, and she's the one who convinced me to make the call."

"I'm glad for whatever led you to make that call." Mark's eyes meet mine, and his are full of passionate fire. "It might have saved my life."

"I know it saved mine." I tilt my chin up and he presses a soft kiss to my mouth that only awakens more desire inside me.

"Oh, thank God!" Lizzie's voice pierces the quiet inside the room. "I thought I was going to have to break up a fist fight in here, but I wasn't sure if it was going to be between Mark and Brian or Reese and Brian."

Dave laughs beside her, and Diane and Paul stand behind them.

"I'm so sorry that I did that outside in front of everyone, Liz," I say. I refrain from saying that I'm not actually sorry I did it.

Lizzie flips a hand in the air. "Forgotten. My wedding planner said we need to get the rehearsal started now that everyone's here. You all ready?"

Brian puts his hand on the small of Kelsey's back to lead her out of the room, and I start to head that way, too. But Mark stops us all in our tracks with his words. "While we're all together and before the craziness begins, I have something to say."

Seven sets of eyes turn on Mark, and he clears his throat. I take a step back to be by his side for whatever he's about to say.

He looks down at me with adoration as he laces his arm around my waist. He clings to me as if he's drawing strength from our connection. He looks over at his sister. "First, congratulations to Lizzie. You'll be a beautiful bride tomorrow, and you're a beautiful bride-to-be tonight." Her eyes shine with tears as her brother speaks. "I'm glad we're all forced in the same room for a happy occasion. I won't go into details, but the past couple months were rough on me. I'm thankful we're all here to celebrate together. I'm thankful Reese is by my side for this, and as hard as it is to admit, I have Brian to thank for that."

He takes a deep breath. "Mom, Dad, what you don't know is that I wasn't hospitalized for exhaustion. I was on a destructive path and didn't give a fuck. Brian recognized that and figured out how to fix it. While I'll never forget that he kept Reese and me apart, I can start the process of forgiving, and I hope you know that I learned forgiveness from the two of you. I hope you'll exercise the same when you think back on everything that's happened."

An awkward beat of quiet passes between all of us after his words before he finishes his speech. "And now I wish I had a glass because that sounded like a toast. It's not. I love you all. Let's go rehearse and then get drunk."

A laugh rises from the group of Fox family members gathered. Mark leans down to press a kiss to my cheek. Lizzie hugs Mark, and I hear her whispered thanks in his ear. She hugs me next, and then she says, "Like he said, let's go rehearse and then get drunk!"

She heads toward the door with Dave. Brian hangs near the door with Kelsey, but before we go through it, we have to face Diane.

"Some speech," she says softly. She gives Mark a hug then looks with anxiety at him. "Are you okay?"

He nods. "I wasn't." He glances briefly over at me before he returns his gaze to his mother. "But then she came back, and now I am."

Diane's eyes fill with tears, and then she does something I never expected.

She reaches out toward me and gives me a hug.

It's not a friendly, warm hug, but it's a start.

"Thank you for whatever you did for him. He was lost, but you found him." Her words are simple, and she stalks out of the room before I have the chance to respond. Paul gives us both a smile, pats his son on the back, then follows his wife out to the patio.

I sigh in relief, but then I spot Brian hanging by the door and unease darts through my chest.

Mark grabs my hand in his and I follow a little behind him as we make our way toward his brother.

Brian clears his throat, all traces of that cocky grin still missing. "Thanks for what you said," he says quietly to his brother.

"Didn't want to fuck up Lizzie's big day."

"You're letting it all go because of Lizzie?" Brian's eyebrows furrow.

Mark shrugs. "Someone has to be the bigger man. You may be a goddamn cocksucker, but you'll always be my annoying little brother." He punches Brian in the arm and then pulls me out the door with him, and I can't help but think how he really does put everybody else first.

What Brian did was unforgivable, yet Mark's heart is so big that he's forgiving him. I don't know that I have the same capacity, but I can certainly learn something from the man I love. And the biggest lesson I've learned is that no one—not even Brian Fox—can come between a man and the woman he's destined to be with.

twenty-four

Lizzie's wedding was beautiful. It went off without a hitch. No bitch slaps, no darting looks of jealousy, no cutting words. Just a celebration of love, life, and family.

It's the day after the wedding—Mark's *one* day off before he has to audition guitarists tomorrow, and I'm lying across his couch with a glass of wine watching some romantic comedy. He said he had some work to do and that he'd join me for the second half of the movie, but it's almost over and I have no idea where he is.

My phone buzzes on the table in front of me, so I pick it up. I have a new Snapchat from Mark Ashton. I smile down at my phone as I unlock it and pull open the app.

It's a picture of Mark. He's not smiling—instead, he's smoldering. The word *destiny* is written in large letters just under his face.

I know what that means, and I don't even care that the rom com on TV only has about four minutes left in it. I run to the bedroom to grab my shoes then race toward the stairs and head up to the roof.

When I get up there, I'm amazed by what's before me.

Landscape lights hang across the top of the roof, lighting the space with a romantic glow. I don't see Mark, but I do see a canvas print propped on an easel right in front of me. It's a huge picture of the two of us, and I recognize it as the first picture we ever took together. It's a Snapchat picture with a filter where the two of us have flowers on our heads. I smile at the image, and then I notice an envelope taped to the easel that says *Reese* on the front of it.

I pull it off and open it, and I find a card inside with Mark's neat handwriting.

The night we met felt a little like destiny, and every day since then has proven that we were inevitable.

I set the card back down and glance around for Mark, but I don't see him. I do, however, see another canvas print of our faces propped on another easel to my right, so I head in that direction. The image on this print was taken just yesterday. It's a candid one the photographer took while we were dancing. I remember Mark had just told me a story about how Ethan once fell out of the top bunk on the bus in the middle of a hookup. I started laughing hysterically at his story, and Mark's laughing, too. He looks happy and light—lighter than I've ever seen him. Even I'm glowing in this one. I open the envelope attached to this easel and read the card.

It's only ever you. From the moment we met, that was the truth.

A big partition that I've never seen before separates me from the other half of the roof. Maybe Mark rented out the space for an upcoming party. I turn around and find another canvas print. It stands as a silhouette against the backdrop of the buildings Mark once used as inspiration for lyrics. I set the card back on the easel then walk toward it. I study the image of us as tears prick behind my eyes.

It's the picture of us right after we got out of the Yukon in Chicago the morning Mark was released from the hospital. I get why he chose this one—it's a pivotal image from an important piece of our history. It was the cause of my "leave of absence" from work, but indirectly it's also the reason why I'm able to travel the country as Penny's assistant. This moment marked a huge turning point in our relationship. There's another card filled with Mark's words.

You allowed me the clean break I didn't know I needed, and now I can look toward the future with you we both deserve.

When I look up from the card, Mark steps out from behind the tall couch. The moment I see him, butterflies dance in my belly. I'm struck with the notion that whatever's about to happen will change my life once again.

I set the card down, and we step toward each other until we meet in the middle. He presses a brief kiss to my lips, and then he takes both my hands in his.

He draws in a deep breath then says, "The other day, my sister said that you fixed me. I didn't know I'd spent my life broken until I met you. I didn't know I needed fixing until I had to live without you. But she's right—you fixed me." The tears that pricked behind my eyes as I looked at the last picture of us spill over onto my cheeks at his words. "I'll never want for anything as long as you're by my side, never need anything except your love, never crave anything except your kiss. And that's why I want you by my side for the rest of my life."

He gets down on his knee, and everything inside me tingles as nerves tighten my chest. He pulls a small, velvet box out of his pocket.

He shakes his head as his green eyes focus on mine. "Life with me won't always be easy, but life isn't easy." His voice shakes with nerves. I've never seen him this riddled with anxiety, and I want to pull him up into my arms to comfort him. "You're the only person in the world I want to face this life with." He flips open the box with shaking hands, and I gasp at the ring inside. "Will you marry me?"

"Yes," I say, nodding as tears freefall down my face. "Of course I will."

As if the nerves fly out of him, he grins with all the boyish charm and charisma I'm used to seeing from him as he slides the ring on my finger. My hand feels heavy as he stands and I fling my arms around him. His mouth crashes down to mine, and that's when I hear a loud crack in the sky.

Fireworks light up the Chicago skyline just as the instrumental music I recognize as the intro to "A Little Like Destiny" starts playing. I pull away from his mouth to see the fireworks, and that's when I also realize that the music I hear isn't coming from speakers. Ethan, Steve, and James are all standing on the roof and the partition that separated us from them is gone. They're playing our song as the fireworks boom and burst into millions of twinkling sparkles and cascades of glittering showers above us. Mark sings the words to me softly as he holds me and we dance on the rooftop toward our future.

one year later

epilogue

After I post a video to Instagram of the empty venue before fans start to arrive, Vinny takes me from the tour bus to the backstage room at the Red Rocks Amphitheater in Denver. Mark stands in the doorway looking like absolute perfection. He's wearing a black shirt and jeans. His dark hair's a flawless disaster, his scruff is that gorgeous length that'll tickle without burning, and his eyes glow a bright green as they land on me.

Before I even step foot into the room, Mark closes the physical distance that separated us for the past couple hours for soundcheck and getting ready for this show. It's always been his dream to play this venue, and tonight Vail goes down in music history. His arms loop around me at the same time his mouth crashes down to mine. I don't even have time to wonder what happened to Vinny as I'm completely consumed by Mark.

His peppermint mouth attacks mine in the sweetest and sexiest way as everything around us melts away into a carnal craving.

He pulls his lips from mine, and I stand in a daze for a beat before I notice that all eyes are on us. Well, almost all eyes. Ethan, who finally admitted he doesn't hate me a couple nights before Mark and I got married, is otherwise engaged in his little corner. I glance around the dressing room, which is really cool. The room is built right around the famous red rocks of this venue, so when I look at one of the walls, I'm actually looking at the side of a mountain.

I don't have much time to focus on the walls, though, because Mark's arm fists my bicep and he leads me over to a door. "Vinny, stand outside the door upstairs." He looks around and his eyes land on Ethan's security guard. "Chuck, stand here. Neither of you lets anyone in for the next five minutes."

He glances at me, the heat and intensity in his eyes knocking me back a step. I immediately know what he plans to do on the other side of this door with me, and I want more than five minutes. "Ten," I demand.

He grins down at me then looks at Vinny and Chuck. "Five to ten minutes. Stay at your post until I come get you."

I giggle, and Vinny opens the door. It's a tunnel with a stairwell, and Vinny takes the steps two at a time before he disappears out the door at the top. The door behind us closes, and we're locked safely in this tunnel with no interruptions for the next five to ten minutes.

I can't help but take in everything around me as we step inside. This is the greatest tunnel I've ever seen in my life. The white walls are coated with black ink, signatures and scribbles and words everywhere. I read a few of the names, recognizing musical greats—names that are on my playlists right beside Vail. Names are written on the flat faces of the stairs, on the handrails, on every available surface—singers and drummers and bassists and guitarists. Musicians and bands.

Mark pulls a black marker out of his pocket and walks over to the wall. He writes his name in his distinct scrawl over some faded ink on the wall.

He walks up a couple steps. I follow behind him and watch as he writes the word *fucked.* He kneels down to one of the steps and writes *his wife, Reese Fox*, and then he stands, walks up a few steps, and finds a small spot on the wall to write *in this tunnel.* He turns around and writes today's date on the opposite wall.

He throws the marker across the room when he finishes writing, and I watch as it bounces off a famous singer's name on the wall before it lands on the floor next to a legendary guitarist's name.

I raise an eyebrow at him. "Oh, you think so, do you?" I ask, my voice a challenge.

"Oh, babe, I definitely think so. I think we need to celebrate our two-month anniversary as newlyweds." Mark takes a self-assured step toward me, and his gaze lands on mine.

A needy ache presses between my legs. "I think you're definitely right."

He laughs, the sweet sound music to my ears after everything we've been through. His hands grip my waist, fingertips digging deliciously into my hips. "We need to have a little talk first, though."

A tremble of fear darts down my spine. "About what?" I ask, forcing a calmness into my voice I don't quite feel.

His fingers move down and cup the outside of the crotch of my jeans. "Skirts and dresses make for much easier quickies than jeans."

I giggle. "So this is a quickie?"

His lips find my neck, his words breathing heat against my skin. "If I could spend the entire night doing this with you, I would. But I have a pretty important gig in an hour."

I giggle. "I have a question for you."

He pulls back and looks at me with alarm.

"One time you said it blows your mind that you couldn't wait to be with me. Why did that blow your mind?"

The alarm in his eyes morphs into something dark and dangerous—but somehow at the same time gentle and full of love. "I've never wanted to put anyone or anything ahead of my music. It's been my first love for the past fifteen or twenty years." He closes his eyes and draws in a breath. "But you're different, Reese. You're first. You'll always be first."

The full force of his words hits me. I can't help myself. I act on complete instinct as I attack.

I go for the mouth first, the place where his words leave his tongue, and I brush that tongue with my own. I know he's going on stage soon and he might have work to do, but this comes first for him.

If it blows his mind, I'm not exactly sure what it does to me.

He kisses me back with a fiery passion. My fingers dip beneath his shirt so I can feel the smooth, silky skin of his back, and then I move my hands between us to treat myself to the ridged muscles of his abdomen. He lets out a soft groan and slips his hands down the back of my jeans to grasp two handfuls of my ass, and I moan.

He grins against my mouth as he knows he has me where he wants me. I'll do anything for him—anything he wants, anything he asks, anything he needs.

He pulls his hands out from my jeans and pulls his shirt over his head. He tosses it on the stairs, probably covering some Grammy award winning band's name, but right now nothing else matters.

My shirt stays on as he works the button of my jeans and pushes them down to my thighs. My hands are busy running over every available inch of his exposed skin, wanting more—craving more, but knowing we're limited to ten short minutes in a tunnel.

"Bend over. Hands covering Josh's name." I look down and see the signature of the lead singer of a rock band. I cover his name with my hands as I was told, my ass up high, the air of the tunnel cooling my exposed, hot flesh.

I hear him rustle around for a second and then feel his swollen head as it moves through my heat. He pushes inside with a low grunt, and I shove back to meet his entry. He holds my hips and stills inside me for a few glorious seconds, and then he starts to really move.

He drives into me, his thrusts punctuated by grunts and gasps as I close my eyes and give into the singular feeling of pleasure only he can deliver.

He pulls out and everything stops for a dizzying minute. "Stand up," he says. "Jeans off."

I do what he says, and he sits on the step and motions for me to straddle him. He fists his dick and guides it in as I slowly lower myself over him. I wrap my arms around his shoulders, and his hands come under my ass to guide me up and down over him. The fullness of him and the feeling of nothing between us is overwhelming. I'm filled not just with him physically, but emotionally. He fills my heart, my mind, my blood, my soul.

That feeling is what pushes me to the finish line. "Oh my God, Mark, I'm coming, I'm coming, I'm coming," I say the words over and over as my body clenches him inside me.

He moves me harder over him and thrusts upward at the same time, finding his own release in sync with mine. My climax is prolonged as we come together too quickly. We allow ourselves a few quiet moments to luxuriate leisurely in a hallway filled with musical memorabilia and now the heady scent of sex and memory of us.

* * *

It's obvious what we just did, but it's not as obvious *where* we just did it. All eyes inspect Mark's flushed cheeks and my rumpled shirt and disheveled hair when we walk into the dressing room.

Including Ethan's. His lady friend is off refilling their drinks, and he speaks first over the quiet that befalls the room at our entrance.

"You find somewhere private or did you just fuck in the hallway?" he asks snidely.

"Fuck off," Mark says.

"Good one."

"He took me somewhere private," I say, allowing my gaze to drift over to Mark. "And it was fantastic."

A wide grin spreads across his face. I catch Morgan's eye, and she winks at me as if to tell me she's proud of me for not allowing Ethan to embarrass us. Ethan's woman returns with their drinks and takes a seat on his lap.

"It's time," Steve says.

Mark nods once, and we all know this means it's time for the pre-game that I still know nothing about. "Ladies, would you please excuse us for a bit?" Mark asks.

Morgan kisses James. Angelique kisses Steve, then Steve kisses baby Adelaide on top of her sweet head filled with blonde curls.

Ethan's woman of the night doesn't budge. He pushes her up off his lap, and I can't help but think he's such a dick. He'll meet the right woman someday, though, just like Mark did.

I hope.

I smile at Mark and turn to follow Morgan and Angelique out the door. Blondie takes off in some other direction, and Vick and the security team head down a hallway that has a sign telling passersby the cafeteria is located that way.

Before I make it out the door, Mark pulls me in for another heated kiss. "I love you," he says into my neck so only I can hear him. It's so intimate and touching that my heart twists.

"I love you, too," I say softly. "Only ever you."

the end

acknowledgments

To my husband first, thank you for reading this series in its original form many, many years ago. Thank you for encouraging me to publish a book and thank you for your constant support and love as I published the first thirteen before I finally got around to rewriting a proper story for these characters. Thank you for whatever the future holds, too, which will include many more stories. Thank you to my little boy for being the sweetest, kindest, and cutest kid ever.

My Vail Tail Fangirls: I love your discussions and GIFs and excitement over this series. I honestly thought the support group for this series would have two people in it and I'd be one of them! I'm overwhelmed by your love for these characters who have lived in my heart for many, many years. Thanks for making the Fangirl group a fun place to be.

Thank you to my ARC team for reading and reviewing, but most of all, thank you for the messages and the love.

Thank you to Stephanie Costa for loving these characters and for believing in them. Thank you for all the great new ideas and for offering to help me manage things when I take on too much. Most of all, thank you for becoming a friend.

Thank you to Jen Wildner for loving these characters and for beta rushing this book.

Thank you to Kelly Werner for beta reading the entire series and for giving me your honesty.

Trenda Tbird Lundin, your masterful skill of editing helped me figure out exactly what I needed to do to make Reese's story complete. Thank you for all your words of advice and encouragement.

Katie Harder-Schauer, thank you for polishing this manuscript and for your support and friendship.

Thank you to the Give Me Books ladies for handling ARCs and release blitzes for this series and the cover reveal and release party for this book. As always, thank you to the bloggers who read and review. Your efforts and hard work are appreciated.

Thank you to you, the reader. I am so grateful that you stuck with Reese through all her indecision and with me through the cliffhangers. I have never loved writing a series more than this one, and I am forever grateful that you took time out of your life to spend it with my characters.

Finally, thank you to Reese Brady, Mark Ashton, and Brian Fox. These characters feel like real people, and I've loved them for a long time. It's surreal to me that they're out there in the world and their story is complete after they lived in my mind for so long. This series was over fifteen years in the making with so many drafts I lost count (I even wrote 70,000 words of *Clean Break* before I archived it and started over...mostly because I wasn't ready to let these characters go yet), and I hope I gave them the ending they deserve. Even though the series is complete, something tells me I'm not quite done with these characters just yet...

xoxo,

Lisa Suzanne

about the author

Lisa Suzanne is a romance author who resides in Arizona with her husband and two kids. She's a former high school English teacher and college composition instructor. When she's not chasing or cuddling her kids, she can be found working on her latest book or watching reruns of *Friends*.

also by Lisa Suzanne

THE POWER TO BREAK

Book 1 in the Invisible Thread Duet featuring Vail's Ethan Fuller

#1 Bestselling Rock Star Romance

TAKE MY HEART

Book 1 in the MFB Standalone Series

#1 Bestselling Rock Star Romance

Made in the USA
Monee, IL
05 January 2024

51290654R00146